DATE DUE

AN AVALON HISTORICAL ROMANCE

THE MARRYIN' KIND
A Morgan Family Romance

Nancy J. Parra

At the ripe old age of twenty-three, Madeline Morgan is resigned to the idea that love and marriage are not for her. Unfortunately, her father disagrees and comes up with an ingenious plan. To curb the love life of his youngest, Robert Morgan proclaims that neither of his younger daughters can marry until Maddie does. This causes a stir and a generous pot is set up for whoever can take Maddie off the market.

Aghast at being hounded by sweaty bachelors anxious to win the pot and her hand, Maddie turns to her brother for help. Her brother's solution is to spread the story that Maddie was pining away for the love of her life, Evan Montgomery, who left for the war and has never returned. Things go from bad to worse when the ladies in town, struck by the romance of long lost love, demand that Maddie's father rescind his proclamation and that the mayor give Maddie the deed to the dilapidated Montgomery ranch.

When Maddie protests that her brother has gone too far, he replies with a shrug and the carefree statement that she needn't worry because after eight years, it's unlikely that any Montgomery would show up.

As luck would have it, two years later Trevor Montgomery returns home to find a beautiful stranger living there, claiming to be his brother's fiancée. A fiancée Trevor wishes were his own. Torn between his loyalty to his brother and the love in his own heart, Trevor works to uncover the truth behind the woman who has stolen more than his family home.

THE MARRYIN' KIND

•

Nancy J. Parra

AVALON BOOKS
NEW YORK

PRINTED IN THE UNITED STATES OF AMERICA
ON ACID-FREE PAPER
BY HADDON CRAFTSMEN, BLOOMSBURG, PENNSYLVANIA

For my wonderful Aunt Marnie Nethercott and all the sisters at Holy Family Convent in Manitowoc, Wisconsin; thank you for jumping up and down with me in excitement. Your wonderful support and the special thank you's that have come my way really make it all worthwhile. Writing these stories wouldn't be nearly as much fun without you.

Chapter One

"It isn't fair!" Beth cried, and flung herself on Madeline's bed.

Maddie looked up from her mending with a patient sigh. Her baby sister Beth had been crying about how unfair the world was practically from the day she learned to talk. "What is it now?"

"Michael went to Papa to ask for my hand in marriage."

"What?!" Maddie stabbed her finger with the needle. The pain made her eyes water. She dropped the petticoat and shoved the offended digit into her mouth. The sharp metallic tang of blood hit her tongue.

Beth grabbed Maddie's pillow and hugged it to her chest. "It was the most romantic thing."

"You're only sixteen and Michael is twenty-one." Maddie couldn't tell if it was the taste of blood or the idea of Beth getting married that soured her stomach.

"Papa turned him down flat." Beth frowned at her. "In fact, he tossed him out the door by his ear."

"Good. That boy does not think with his head." Relieved, Maddie pressed on the wound until the blood stopped. It wouldn't do to get a stain on Amelia's newest undergarment.

1

"He absolutely loves me," Beth said with confidence. "He told me so himself and then he kissed me."

"He kissed you?! He should be ashamed."

"Don't be such an old pooh. It was quite lovely."

"You're too young. You need to finish school and mature a little before you even think about boys and marriage."

"I have to do something," Beth said, and sat up straight. "I refuse to be an old spinster like you."

"Beth!" The comment lashed at Maddie's heart. To begin with she was not old. Why, just last month she had had her twenty-third birthday. That was far from old. Secondly she chose to be single. There was something wonderfully liberating about not having to be at a man's beck and call.

"Now all of my hopes of ever marrying are gone," Beth said with so much devastation and drama that tears welled up in her sparkling blue eyes.

"Nonsense," Maddie said and put her work aside. She went over to her baby sister and brushed the hair away from Beth's face. "Give yourself a year. Things will change."

"It's hopeless," Beth said and turned her face into the pillow. "Papa has declared that none of us can marry before you."

"What?"

Beth pulled her head up off the pillow. "You heard me. He has announced to the whole town that Amelia and I are unavailable until after you get married."

"That's ridiculous," Maddie said, fear climbing up her throat. She jumped up and paced the floor. Her muslin skirts whooshed softly around her ankles as she walked. "I don't ever intend to marry and Papa knows it."

Beth knelt on the bed beside her. "But you must get married," she wailed. "You simply must or I will have to spend my whole life alone."

"He can't mean it," Maddie said. "I'll go talk to him."

"It won't make any difference. He's already announced it."

"He should have spoken to me first," Maddie said, swallowing her panic. "Now he'll have to take back his announcement."

"He won't," Beth warned. "He was very serious."

Maddie went straight into action. It was nearly 3 P.M. and her father would be in his den working on the finances. It was a good time to face him down. She formed her arguments as she went down the stairs. She would tell her father that he could keep up the charade for a time until Amelia and Beth were old enough to marry. Then he would have to take back his announcement, because she was not marrying . . . ever.

Maddie walked down the hall toward her father's office when there was a knock on the front door. "I'll get it," Maddie called to Mrs. Poole the housekeeper. Maddie opened the door to find Stuart Bixley standing there with wilted flowers drooping over his bony hand. "Good afternoon, Stuart," Maddie said.

"Mmmmadeline," Stuart said. He was nearly as tall as she was, but so thin that he appeared to be a stick figure, except for a prominent Adam's apple.

She waited for him to explain himself, but his gaze simply shifted from one point over her head to another. "Are you here to see Papa?" she asked finally, in hopes of coaxing some purpose out of him.

"Umm, nope," he replied.

She waited another moment, but he still did not speak. She glanced at the small watch pinned to her chest. If he didn't hurry she would miss her opportunity. Papa went out to his club every afternoon at four. "I'm sorry, Stuart, you're going to have to tell me who it is you wish to see."

"Oh, uh, I came to see you," he said and thrust the flowers toward her. "Um, these are for you."

"Thank you," she said and took the bouquet. "But I had no idea you were coming to call. You see, I'm right in the middle of something. Perhaps you can come back later."

"Uh, okay," he said with a look of relief. "I'll come back later."

"Good day, then," Maddie said.

"Good day." He simply stood there shuffling from one foot to the other. When he didn't leave, she figured she'd have to spell it out.

"Well, thank you for the flowers. Next time send your card around first. I'll let you know if I have any free time. Good day."

"Good day." He seemed fixated on a spot off her right shoulder.

Maddie shook her head and shut the door in his face. She waited until she heard him turn and walk off the porch.

"What was that all about?"

"I have no earthly idea," Maddie said to Mrs. Poole. "Here, please put these poor things out of their misery." She shoved the badly wilted bouquet into the housekeeper's capable hands. "I need to have a talk with Papa and I need to have it now."

She knocked on the door to his study. "Come in." Maddie stormed the fortress. Inside, her father sat at his big mahogany desk, his feet propped up on the top, and his face hidden behind a newspaper.

"Papa, Beth just told me the most ridiculous fairytale."

"What is it now?" he asked and turned the page.

"She told me that you announced to the whole town that Beth and Amelia could not marry until I did." She plopped down into a winged-back chair that faced his desk. "Is that not the silliest thing you have ever heard?"

"It's not silly, Madeline. It's true." He casually flipped another page.

"What?!" She leapt up, unable to control the panic in her voice. "Why would you tell everyone that I must marry first?"

"It is a reasonable request," her father said through his

newspaper. "You are the oldest. Some might even say it was customary."

"Papa, please, you know I am not so foolish as to run off and marry the first man who asked me."

"Precisely," he said and folded his paper. "You are a wise woman, Madeline. You have my highest confidence that you will resolve the matter to my satisfaction."

"If I must marry it won't be to my satisfaction," she replied, and paced his office. "Besides, I don't see you worrying about Robert and he's two years older than I am."

"He's also a man," Papa said. "A man has the natural right to choose how to live his life."

"A woman doesn't?" she asked aghast.

"A woman needs a man to protect her and to run the household," her father said firmly. "I've decided when I die there will be no spinsters left in my house."

Maddie looked into her father's blue eyes. "I am already passed marrying age. Some might even say it will be most difficult to get rid of me."

Her father snorted at the thought. "You are as beautiful as your mother was. Besides, I happen to know there has already been one man at our door looking to lure you out."

"Stuart Bixley," she said, disgusted. "Really. I won't have it."

"Well, I will and I'm the papa. Now, go be a good girl and enjoy the attention."

A full month later, Maddie had still not been able to talk her father out of his ridiculous proposal. Even her three brothers had told him how crazy he was, but Papa had stood firm. Maddie's life was in ruins. It seemed that there was a large group of men in town all desperate for Beth's hand. They had gotten together and put up a substantial reward for the man who married Maddie. It didn't matter who won the pot, only that Maddie was married and quickly.

The only thing she could do to stop the madness was not

be home when they called. So Maddie had taken to visiting her friends, or the sick, or anyone who happened to be home.

She had just left the O'Reily's house when she caught sight of yet another sweaty, nervous bachelor with flowers in his hand, bearing down upon her. She was lucky that she had seen him when there was still enough distance between them that she could manage to avoid him by slipping through the church and down a back alley.

Alone at last, she found a stump in a small grove where she was able to sit and enjoy the fresh air and peace. She shook her head. The whole idea was beyond her. Years ago, she had settled herself to the fact that she would never marry. With so many boys off to war, her father hadn't worried about her state of singleness. Her sisters had been very young and Maddie had been free.

A single woman could own property and manage her own affairs. A married woman on the other hand was little more than property to her husband. Maddie hated the idea of being on par with a man's horse.

She sighed and leaned back against a tree. Her father kept telling her to enjoy the attention. What was the point? All the men chasing her weren't in love with anything but the money that was waiting for the man brave enough to claim her.

She hugged her knees and shook her head. It wasn't that she was difficult. No, she was simply . . . astute. She wanted to be able to live life as she saw fit. Most important, she refused to sell herself to the first man who professed to love her.

Maddie let out a sound of disgust at the thought of love. As far as she was concerned true love was only found in fairytales. She wasn't like Beth, willing to give her heart willy-nilly to anyone who showed the least bit of interest.

She had put many hours of thought into the idea of marriage. Most girls married young and went straight from their father to their husband. They fooled themselves into thinking it was love, but it wasn't. How could they love a man twenty years older than them?

Maddie stood and picked a single white flower. She put it in her hair. She realized her father thought she was simply too educated, and perhaps she was. Perhaps Sir Walter Scott and the poet Byron had put unattainable thoughts in her head.

She sighed. If she was to be truthful, what she really wanted was a small home of her own. One with a garden just big enough to give her the fresh vegetables she loved. Maybe it would have a small fireplace that she could sit next to and do her stitches.

She shook her head. All her dreams were of her alone. There was never a man bursting in, making demands. How ever was she to marry when all she wanted was to be alone?

"Hi, sis, are you hiding out?"

She turned to see her older brother Robert coming toward her. She and Robert had always been close. In fact, he was the only one who could find her in the forest. He was the only one who knew her that well.

"Robert, what brings you out here?"

"I'm hiding too," he said with a sad grin, and leaned against a tree. "When the suitors couldn't find you they started trailing me."

She glanced around. "They didn't follow you here did they?"

"Of course not. You know I'm better than that."

She relaxed. "This thing with Papa is simply ridiculous. I can't believe he's actually insisting."

"He only wants what's best for you," Robert said. "Truly, I spoke to him about it."

"How can a gang of thin, mealy mouthed men be what is best for me?" She crossed her arms around her waist. "Have you seen who has come courting?"

"I don't blame you for being a little scared. I've seen the bachelors and I think I'm scared."

She laughed at his humor, then sobered. "What am I going to do?"

"What is it you want to do?"

"I've been thinking about that," she said. "The truth is, I would love to have a place of my own. Do you realize that widows have the greatest benefit? They can own their own property and they have neither father nor husband to contend with."

"Too bad you have to be a wife before you can be a widow," Robert said wryly.

"Yes. Too bad I didn't have the good sense to marry before the war. The man might actually be dead by now."

"Blood thirsty and morbid," Robert said with a grin. "A gal after my own heart."

"Stop it," she said and slugged his arm. "You know what I meant."

"Yes, I do, and I do believe you have hit upon the perfect solution."

"What, that I marry a dead man?"

"Something like that. Come with me. I want to show you something."

She took her brother's hand and he pulled her through the forest. The woods opened up into a clearing on its western edge. In the middle of the clearing stood a small house. It was beautiful at one time. She could tell from the faded green shutters and white-washed siding. There was a small fairytale porch with roses, now wild, twining up the posts.

"Who would abandon such a beautiful place?" she asked. "Surely fairies play here."

Robert laughed. "Wait until you see the inside." He strode up the porch and shouldered the door open. The inside was neat and tidy and practically Maddie's dream. They stepped into a small kitchen with a large fireplace.

Behind it was a parlor with a settee and a rocking chair, table and lamps, and an entire wall full of books.

"Oh my gosh," Maddie said, and gravitated toward the wall. "Books. All these lovely books . . . abandoned." She ran her fingers along the spines. "Sir Walter Scott, Shakespeare, and Byron . . ."

Robert leaned against the doorjamb and crossed his arms. "The collection belonged to Pricilla Montgomery."

Concerned, she turned to her brother. "Where is Pricilla? Something awful must have happened for her to abandon these beautiful books."

"She died a few years back."

"How?"

"Illness took her shortly after her boys enlisted."

"Did they know their mother died?"

"Trevor came back and saw that she had a proper funeral, but Evan never returned."

"What happened to them? It's clear no one lives here now."

Robert shrugged. "Rumor has it that both boys died in the war."

Suddenly Maddie knew where her brother's thoughts were going. "What are you saying?"

"I'm saying you go to Papa and tell him of your unrequited love for Evan Montgomery. Tell him that you and Evan were secretly engaged before he left for the war and that is why you wish to remain single."

"I couldn't."

He lifted one corner of his mouth in a wry grin. "Why not? It's the perfect solution."

"How is it perfect? I have never met Evan Montgomery."

"Not a problem. Evan has been missing since before his mother died. That was six years ago. He's more than likely dead, leaving you a practical widow."

"What if he isn't dead?"

"It could be years before we find out and then I'll be here to help."

"Help how?"

"Evan and I went to school together. I will explain your predicament to him. Evan loves a good joke. He'll be happy to play along. Maybe even break your heart. I can see it now. All the ladies will stand with you. You will be devastated. Surely Papa couldn't think of putting you through that ordeal again. Trust me. You'll be home free."

"I don't know."

"I'll start the tale around town about how you and Evan were secretly in love before he left for the war."

"But we weren't."

"No one would know that but you. I can write up a few love letters. Nothing fancy."

"And . . ."

"And then you could spread the tale of how much in love you are . . . How no one else but Evan will do."

"I can't—"

"It's not really a lie," Robert said with a smile. "You have told me time and again that you have no desire to marry. Simply tell him it's because of Evan. Then, until Evan Montgomery actually shows up, you will be considered off limits to the rest of the male population."

"I don't know. I couldn't lie like that."

"Fine, I'll let the suitors know where you are," Robert said and turned as if to leave the house.

"No," she nearly shouted. "You wouldn't be that cruel."

"It's not my choice, it's yours," he said. "All you have to do is go to Papa and tell him why you don't want to get married—ever."

Maddie chewed her bottom lip. "It sounds deceptively simple. What if something goes wrong?"

"What could possibly go wrong?"

* * *

Within two days, Maddie had the answer to her question. She was in the parlor arranging the many bouquets from the suitors when there was a knock at the door.

Maddie opened it to find Mrs. Selis and Mrs. Lance standing there with looks of deep concern in their eyes. "Maddie, we just heard," Mrs. Selis said, and pushed her way into the house. Blanche Selis had been trying to catch Maddie's father's eye for years. It was clear that it wasn't her father Blanche was interested in. It was what her father owned.

"Horrible, simply horrible," Mrs. Lance said, and followed Blanche inside. She brushed away the oversized plume that threatened to fall out of her hat. "Don't worry dear, we will speak to your father at once."

"I beg your pardon?" Maddie said as the two ladies peered nosily down the hallway toward her father's den.

"It's okay, dear," Blanche said, and patted Maddie's arm. "We're here now. We will take care of everything."

"Take care of what?"

"Why your engagement of course," Mrs. Lance said. "Your darling brother, let your secret slip."

"My secret?"

"Yes, about your engagement to Evan Montgomery," Blanche said and sighed. "What a romantic story, and now your father wants you to forget all that and marry someone else. Well, that just isn't right."

"It just isn't," Mrs. Lance parroted.

"What with your dear mother buried all these long years, the ladies of Boltonville have decided that we should represent you in this matter. It's clear your father does not have your best interests in mind."

"Quite clear," Mrs. Lance said.

"We know he's home, dear. We saw him come in from riding. Now, if you will kindly announce us, we will get this matter taken care of right away."

Maddie's heart leapt into her throat. What exactly had

Robert done? "Mrs. Selis, Mrs. Lance," Maddie started. "Thank you for thinking of me, but I really don't think that you need to speak to my father about this."

"It's okay, dear, your brother told us how you're torn between pleasing your father and keeping your own love's light lit." Blanche smiled sharply and moved down the hallway like a battleship ploughing through the sea. "Not to worry, we have it all in hand." She waved a gloved hand at Maddie who stood there open-mouthed.

"Yes, all in hand," Mrs. Lance said.

Then the two women marched themselves right into her father's den. Unannounced. It was horrifying.

Mrs. Poole, the housekeeper, came around the corner from the kitchen. "What is it, Madeline? You look as if you've just been told your best friend has died."

"Oh, no," Maddie said, her tone as grim as she felt inside. "This is much worse than that. The Mrs. Selis and Lance have come to speak to father about me."

"Oh, dear."

"You'd better fix a tray for tea," Maddie said as she stared at the closed den door. "Or better yet, something stronger."

"I'll bring it right in," Mrs. Poole said.

Maddie swallowed the sudden urge to run and hide. Instead she opened the door to find her father staring out the window, while Blanche lectured him on the proper way to deal with Maddie's tender heart.

Over the next two weeks, things went from bad to worse. The ladies brigade needed something to do and Maddie became just that. One by one, the ladies visited her father until he finally caved. He rescinded his declaration that Maddie should marry, and instead announced that she was already engaged.

Throughout all this, Maddie's father refused to talk to her. He was torturously quiet whenever Maddie was around. So much so that she took to leaving the room whenever he was near, which played right into the ladies' hand.

They decided that it was only right that Maddie move out to the Montgomery house. Horrified, Maddie told the ladies that she would not leave her father's house, but the brigade was firm in its plans. Despite Maddie's protests, they petitioned the mayor, who saw the seven hundred signatures as a sign, and declared that for the peace and wellbeing of Boltonville, Madeline Morgan should move into the Montgomery homestead.

Of course the men were happy as well. They were now free to court Maddie's sisters without having to pay up the impossibly large coffer that had been offered to get Maddie out of the way.

Robert was no help with the matter. He simply grinned his cocky grin at Madeline and helped her move her few possessions into the Morgan home.

"What have you done?" Maddie hissed between her teeth.

"I told you it would be perfect. I had no idea they would actually declare the place yours."

"This does not belong to me," she said, and waved at the dusty furniture that filled the cabin. "It's not right."

"It does so belong to you," Robert said. "I saw the official declaration. Why, the mayor practically handed you the deed."

Maddie stomped her foot in frustration. "Robert, I can't do this."

"Why not? It's perfect. The ladies wanted to help you, and look at what they've accomplished." He set her trunk down in the kitchen and brushed his hands off. "I must say when I do something, I do it right."

"You made up the most preposterous tale I've ever heard. I can't believe they believed it."

"The ladies wanted a little romance," he said and

shrugged. "So I gave it to them. Look, Maddie, since the war, the ladies needed a cause. That's why they rallied around your story. They would be heartbroken if you told them it was all a lie."

"But it was."

"A little white lie," he said. "Think of Mrs. Addlestone. She's nearly seventy-two years old. It would kill her to find out that her romantic story wasn't true."

"I suppose you think I should keep this up until the old dear dies."

"It wouldn't hurt. She'll go to her grave thinking about how she helped you out in your time of need."

"It will be years before they all die. Mrs. Selis is only forty-four."

"She is a pretty widow, too. I don't know why Papa doesn't think about sparking her."

"Oh, you are too much," Maddie said with a frown. "Go, get out of here before I hurt you."

Robert grinned and ducked as she swung at him. "I love you, Maddie."

"Sure you do. Look what you've done to me."

"I've given you exactly what you wished for. Isn't that enough?"

"What do I do if the Montgomerys come riding back into town?"

"That isn't going to happen."

"What if it does?"

"Don't worry, Maddie. I'll be the first one here to greet them. We'll explain what happened and all have a good laugh."

"Papa's already not talking to me."

"Don't worry, he'll relax in time."

Maddie sat down on one of the kitchen chairs. "He'll kill us."

"All the more reason not to upset the apple cart." Robert

looked around. "It really is a nice place. I think you'll be happy here."

Maddie glumly planted her elbows on the table. "I sure hope you're right."

"Of course I'm right," Robert said with a grin. "I'm a Morgan, aren't I?"

Maddie didn't answer him. She had heard that the Montgomerys were about as uncivilized as the Morgans.

Maybe she'd get lucky. Maybe the Montgomerys would never come home.

Chapter Two

A cold rain fell on the forest, drenching Trevor Montgomery to the bone, and putting a damper on his melancholy mood. It was the end of October and fall had found its way into the Wisconsin countryside.

The scent of dying leaves and the sharp warning of winter cold welcomed him back to the homestead. His mother had been dead for nearly eight years. The war had been over for six. Trevor wondered if the old place still stood, or if time and nature had reclaimed it.

He rubbed the ache in his right leg. A bullet had torn through his muscle in one of the last battles of the war. He knew the pain would haunt him the rest of his life. Sometimes late at night he still heard the screams of the dead and dying, still smelled gore on the air, and wondered if the madness would ever leave him.

He rubbed the ache and nudged his horse forward. It had taken him six years to come home, six years of wandering, waiting for the blackness to leave his heart, the stain of sorrow and death to leave his soul. About a month ago, he'd been in a saloon in Memphis and he'd realized that he was bone tired and going nowhere. He needed to go home.

Between the rain, the trees and the season, the sky was black as midnight and it was only 6 P.M. He shivered. Whatever longing drove him home would not be appeased tonight. If he was lucky, he'd find a few logs to start a fire in the fireplace. He'd be luckier still if he didn't have to kick the critters out of the chimney first.

He rounded a corner and the meadow opened up before him. Astonished at the sight, he stopped the horse and stared. The homestead was brightly lit. Thick white smoke curled out of the chimney. Pumpkins rested on the porch and what looked like mums grew in the flowerbeds along the edge.

A solid sense of déjà vu swept over him. It looked as if his mother still lived there. As if she knew he was coming and had a thick warm stew sitting on the stove waiting for him.

He imagined finding her at the door, smiling and welcoming him home. He shook the thought off quickly. His mother had been dead for many years. His brother had disappeared early on in the war. It was rumored that he had died in the mountains of West Virginia, but no body had been found.

Perhaps, just perhaps, it had only been a rumor. Perhaps Evan had come home.

Trevor approached the house with hope and caution. He dismounted and drew his horse toward the barn. If Evan was home, then he must have married, for the flowers and pumpkins were sure signs a woman lived there.

Trevor opened the barn door. Inside was dark and warm. A lantern sat near the door and he lit it and got a good look. The barn was relatively small, but the loft was packed with fresh hay. One of the stalls held a milk cow, another held a mare. The third stall was empty. He led his horse there, took off his saddle, and fed, watered and brushed the animal. It had been a long journey.

Trevor was tired and in pain. He glanced again at the

cow as he exited the barn. She was fat and sassy. It seems his baby brother had done well for a dead man.

Trevor eased his aching shoulders and blew out the lamp. The sharp scent of lamp oil and smoke filled the air. He put the lantern back in its place by the door and stepped out into the frigid night air.

He wondered briefly why his brother hadn't contacted him. Why no one had let him know that he had family alive and well. His stomach rumbled and he figured those were questions that would soon be answered.

He made his way through the boggy yard and up onto the porch. There was a rag rug near the door and he stopped long enough to wipe his feet before he opened the door. With a quick knock he entered the house. "Hello the house."

"Take another step and I will shoot you." The sound of a determined woman hit him at the same time as the warmth of the interior caressed his cheek.

Trevor raised his hands and blinked as his eyes tried to adjust to the bright lamplight. "I'm Trevor Montgomery and I live here."

Cold silence, and then the sound of a rifle being cocked met his announcement. He turned toward the sound. Off to his right stood a creature straight out of his dreams. Long dark hair ran loose and free over small shoulders. A pale heart-shaped face held an expression of doubt and determination.

Midnight-blue eyes were surrounded by thick black lashes. A small elegant nose and soft welcoming mouth gave her the look of an angel. She wore a long white cotton nightgown and pale blue robe tied around a narrow waist. The outfit gave him ample view of curves that were not enhanced by corset or hoop.

"I'm Trevor Montgomery," he replied slowly. "Evan will vouch for me."

"Evan's busy."

"Look, I've come a long way. If I wanted to rob you I wouldn't have my hands up in the air."

"You're carrying a gun."

"Most men do."

"What was your mother's name?"

"Pricilla."

"Where is she now?"

"She's buried out by the big oak tree," he said.

"That doesn't prove anything," she said. "You could have scouted out the place."

"If I wanted to rob you, I wouldn't have wiped my boots before I came in."

She glanced down at his feet. He followed her gaze and was relieved to see that he'd managed to wipe off most of the barn muck on the rug.

"Like I said, I'm Trevor Montgomery. This is my home."

She glanced up at him, indecision and something close to guilt flashed across her face. "Give me your gun."

"If it makes you feel safer," he said, and reached for his six shooter.

"Slowly," she said. "And keep your other hand up in the air."

He did what she asked, releasing the fastener on his holster. He took off his gun belt and placed it gently on the kitchen table. Then put his hand back in the air. Rainwater ran off his slicker and pooled on the floor around his feet. His stomach growled.

He'd been right in his initial assessment of the house. The kitchen was warm and filled with the homey smells of stew and fresh bread. "I'm sorry if I startled you."

She kept the rifle high and pointed at his heart as she reached for his gun. When it was safely on her side of the table, she lowered the rifle so that it now pointed way below his heart. "I'm not used to men bursting into my home."

"I guess I was expecting a warmer welcome."

"You've been gone a long time."

"Eight years," he acknowledged.

"Everyone thought you were dead."

He sent her a wry grin. "I'm not."

She seemed to make a decision then. "I suppose you haven't eaten."

He didn't comment.

She blew out a breath. "You can hang your slicker near the door. I've got some stew and some bread."

"So, it's safe to put my hands down?" he asked, looking pointedly at her rifle.

She pointed the gun toward the floor. "It's safe," she said. "As long as you don't do anything stupid."

"Right." He took off his hat and his slicker. The black leather was waxed to a high sheen and the water simply rolled off with each movement. "If you have a rag, I'll mop up the floor," he offered. His ma had been particular about her floors and from the look of them so was she.

She tossed a rag his way. "Thanks." He hid his grin. She hadn't protested that she would take care of it. No, she fully expected him to pitch in and clean up after himself. He wondered if she knew how telling that was.

"It'll help if you take off your boots," she said.

"Further proof that I'm not here to rob you," he said as he pulled off his boots.

She raised an eyebrow at him. He lifted his boots in the air. "It's tough to make a fast escape in stocking feet, especially with that cold rain coming down."

"There's soap near the sink so you can wash up."

He walked over to the sink and pressed the pump until fresh cold water splashed out. "I remember when my father put this sink in," he said conversationally. "It was a birthday present for my ma. I've never seen her so tickled. It was something special not to have to haul water from the outside well."

"It's one of the things I like best about the house," she

said as she set a bowl of steaming stew on the table. He washed up, wiped his hands on a nearby towel and sat down at the table.

She placed a plate of sliced bread beside him and a small bowl of fresh butter. "Eat. I'm going to make coffee."

"This looks wonderful," he said and spooned up some of the stew. It was full-bodied and rich on his tongue. Peppered pieces of beef, roasted potatoes and carrots joined together to delight his tongue. He hadn't tasted anything that good in years. "Tastes wonderful," he added.

"Thank you," she said, and sat down at the table across from him. He noted that the rifle now resting on the pie safe was never out of reach and mentally shrugged. If he was a woman alone, he'd be smart enough to do the same thing.

"Evan's not here, is he?"

"I expect him any moment."

He let the lie slide. Her nightclothes made it clear she was alone for the evening. He buttered a slice of bread and feasted on it. "Delicious."

"Thank you."

"You're welcome. You know you have the advantage," he said and took another bite.

"Because I have the guns?"

"No, because you know who I am, but I have no idea who you are."

A pink blush raced over her cheeks. "I'm Madeline."

"Madeline." He liked the sound of it on his tongue. "You're a good cook, Madeline."

There was a pounding at the door and Madeline jumped up to answer it. Trevor wondered who else was out on this dark cold night.

Madeline pulled the door open and a young woman burst in with the wind and the rain. "Maddie, you'll never guess what I heard." She pushed the hood of her cloak off her head to reveal dark hair and wind-kissed cheeks. "Rudy

Harrison said he was headed toward the saloon when he saw—"

She stopped short and gaped at Trevor. "Hello."

"Hello," Trevor said and stood up.

The younger gal's blue eyes widened. "Wow." She glanced at Madeline then back at him. "I'm sorry, I didn't know you had company."

"Beth Morgan, this is Trevor Montgomery," Madeline said, and took the young woman's cloak. She hung it up next to Trevor's duster. She strategically placed a towel on the floor to catch the drips that ran off the garments.

Beth's sweet face lit up. She held out her hand. "Oh, my, it's true. Evan's brother has returned. What a surprise."

Trevor took her gloved hand and bowed over it. The leather was cold and damp from the weather. "The surprise is all mine."

She giggled and took her hand back. "I bet you were surprised to find Maddie here."

He glanced at Madeline. She pulled the belt of her robe tighter around her waist. "I think we startled each other."

"Sit, sit," Beth said engagingly and pulled up a chair. "Don't let me come between you and Maddie's supper. My sister sure can cook." She sat and took off her gloves.

Trevor agreed, and eased his sore body back into the chair. "I was just asking Madeline to tell me how she came to be in my family home."

Madeline moved over to the stove and made a show of fixing the coffee. Beth's face lit up and she leaned toward him. "It's the most romantic thing," she said with excitement. "It seems that just before the war started Maddie and your brother Evan fell in love."

Trevor narrowed his eyes. "Before the war."

"It was all hush hush. Evan knew he would be going off to war, and he asked Maddie to marry him. So, you see, Maddie is your brother's fiancée."

"They're not married?" Trevor said. It didn't make sense.

The war had been over for years. Madeline was living in his family home. Why weren't they married?

"Of course not silly," Beth said and put her hand on Trevor's arm. "Maddie's still waiting for Evan to return."

"Evan hasn't come home?"

"No," Beth said. "It's quite sad really. It's been years and years and still Maddie waits for him."

Trevor glanced at Madeline. She didn't look the type to pine away on long lost love. Something wasn't quite right.

"Still forbidden love." Beth sighed. "So romantic."

"Forbidden?"

"Oh, yes. Papa would have had a fit. Maddie was only fifteen at the time," she said. "Of course, Evan was eighteen so the difference in age wasn't so great. Anyway, Maddie never let another man court her. People thought maybe there was something wrong with her."

"Beth!" Madeline gasped.

"But there wasn't," Beth was quick to say. "You see, she was secretly pining away for your brother."

Trevor frowned. The whole thing sounded suspicious. He glanced at Maddie. There was clearly nothing wrong with her. Any man in his right mind wouldn't mind coming home to her. The house was clean and well kept. Why hadn't she married?

Trevor knew that Evan was a charmer, but not enough that a beautiful woman would put her life on hold indefinitely. It was time to ask some pointed questions.

"Funny," Trevor said. "Evan never said anything about a romance."

"He wouldn't have," Beth went on. "He knew how crazy our papa was. If Papa found out, he'd have taken a shotgun to your brother."

"So, where did you meet?" Trevor asked Madeline, who still bustled about the stove. "It's clear he didn't walk you to church or take you out driving where others could see."

"Oh, I hadn't thought to ask that," Beth said and turned

toward Maddie. "But it is a good question. Where did you meet?"

Maddie turned with a tray of mugs, cream, and sugar which she put on the table. "Evan was in our brother Robert's class at school."

"Ah," Beth said and turned back to Trevor. "That's it then. Evan must have come over to our house to visit with Robert."

"Robert Morgan?" Trevor hated to admit it but the name sounded familiar.

"They were fast friends," Maddie said and served the coffee.

"Of course," Beth said and clapped her hands. "Evan must have told everyone he was going places with Robert, when in reality he was meeting Maddie." She smiled dreamily. "I bet you took long walks in the woods, didn't you?"

"Well, to be honest—"

"Of course you did. One of the ladies at the Boltonville Ladies Brigade remembers seeing you strolling with Evan in the apple orchard. She said you were so obviously in love it made her heart hurt." Beth leaned toward Maddie. "That's why the ladies were so supportive."

"How were the ladies supportive?" Trevor asked and took the coffee Maddie offered him.

"Why, when they found out that Papa was forcing her to see other men, they led a petition drive," Beth said with satisfaction. "I believe Maddie still has the petition. Don't you, Maddie? Why don't you go get it and show it to Trevor." Beth paused and covered her mouth in horror. "I'm sorry, I called you Trevor without asking. Is it all right that I call you, Trevor? I realize we just met, but, well, we are practically family, after all."

"Practically," Trevor muttered. He had warmed up in the heat of the kitchen. His stomach was full of soothing food.

Yet, he still hurt. The pain in his bones was making this strange tale hard to follow. "What is this about a petition?"

"The ladies petitioned the mayor to have Maddie move into this house," Beth said.

"Really. Why?" Trevor rubbed his temples.

"Because the homestead had been abandoned for four years. It was becoming a local eyesore."

"So, the ladies of Boltonville petitioned the mayor to give the place to your sister."

"Yes, sort of," Beth said. "You see, when they found out that Maddie was secretly engaged to your brother Evan, well, the ladies went straight to Papa and demanded that he release Maddie from her need to marry."

"Maddie had a need to marry?"

"Well, of course she did," Beth said. "You see Papa had declared that Maddie must marry before Amelia—she's our other sister."

"Of course."

"Before Amelia and I could marry. Which was a silly proclamation anyway, but Papa had made it. Of course, he didn't have any idea about Maddie's secret engagement when he made his proclamation."

"I bet he didn't."

"Well, the ladies convinced Papa to rescind his word and let Maddie free. Which he did, of course."

"Of course."

"The ladies were so excited about their victory, that they decided Maddie was grown up enough to be out on her own."

Trevor let his gaze fall over the very grown up Maddie. She stirred cream and sugar into her coffee mug with the attention of a scholar. He noted the high color on her lovely cheekbones, and the fact that she remained silent while her sister chatted on.

Trevor wondered what was going through Maddie's mind. There was something behind this story, he just knew it. If he weren't in pain from the trip and the cold night, he might be able to ferret out what exactly was going on here.

"So," Beth said with glee. "The ladies brigade started a petition and got everyone in town to sign it. Then they took it to the mayor."

"They took it to the mayor."

"Yes, you can imagine his surprise."

"Hmm," Trevor said and took a sip of black coffee. "Yes, I can." The coffee tasted unusually good, flavorful and smooth. Dark enough to call it coffee, and yet not nearly as bitter as the trail coffee he was used to drinking.

"Well," Beth continued. "The mayor looked the petition over, saw that there were nearly seven hundred signatures, and agreed that the townspeople surely couldn't be wrong about such a thing. So he declared that Maddie should move into your homestead and restore the place until such time as Evan came home."

"What would happen then?" Trevor asked. Curiosity had gotten the better of him.

"Why, they'd get married of course, don't be silly." She glanced at her sister. "Really Maddie, you should get him the petition. It would be so much easier to explain."

"Yes, Madeline," Trevor found himself saying. "Do get the petition. I'm curious to see it." He was curious. He had grown up in Boltonville, and in all his days of living here he'd never once heard of the mayor putting the care of a farm in a woman's name. It had to be one hell of a petition.

"Fine," Maddie said with raw dignity, and stood. "I'll get the petition."

He watched her go. She moved with appealing grace. Everything about her drew his attention. It was all wrong. If what her sister said was true, then this woman belonged to his brother. If it wasn't true, then she was a little liar out to steal away his family home.

Either way, the last thing he should be feeling is desire as he watched her walk away.

Chapter Three

Madeline's heart raced with embarrassment, regret and just a niggling of pure unadulterated fear. She knelt beside her bed and pulled a box out from under it. It had been two years since Robert had started the rumor about her fairytale romance with Evan Montgomery. Two years since the ladies had practically moved her into the farmstead themselves.

The first few months had been nerve wracking. She had been certain that Evan would come home at any moment and tell the town the truth. But it never happened. She had worked hard to restore the homestead to make up for the fact that she lived there under false pretenses, and the townspeople were happy.

So happy, in fact, they had asked Maddie to speak to the ladies brigade on the finer points of gardening and home repair.

But Maddie knew the truth. It ate away at her. Over time, she vowed that, should anyone question her, she would tell the truth, but no one ever did. They all seemed happy that she was practically widowed. The suitors went joyfully back to the saloon and Maddie had found the peace she wanted. Best of all she had the freedom to be herself.

Soon, no one even thought about the rumor. Even her father had settled into the story. He often sent her sisters or brothers over when he had enough of them and wanted them out of the house.

After two years, Maddie was happy for the company. There was one thing she had learned in living her life of freedom. Being alone was a very lonely thing. Some days she was so lonely, she went into town on errands that didn't need to be done.

A few months ago, she had started tutoring a few of the boys in town. It gave her a little pin money, but most of all, it gave her someone to talk to.

Loneliness was nothing compared to what Maddie faced tonight. Trevor Montgomery had come home and the story of her romance appeared awfully thin. She had seen the look on his face when Beth started talking. It was clear he didn't think Evan would have asked her to marry him.

Her sister's words rang through her mind. *They thought maybe something was wrong with her.* Maddie swallowed the horrible thought that they had been right.

No, she told herself. She had simply not found a man who loved her. Well, that wasn't true—Stuart swore he loved her, when he was able to get the words out. She sighed. Maddie had never loved a man. That was the truth. Maybe there was something wrong with her.

She pulled out the box and fumbled through the papers until she found the small group of petition letters rolled and tied with a pink ribbon. She pulled them out along with the certificate of custodianship.

How she could have let the townspeople talk her into this foolishness was beyond her. She knew the ladies were simply in love with the idea of unrequited love. They each imagined how romantic it was that she would have saved herself all these years. It was the romance that they reacted to, not Maddie's goodness.

Maddie blew out a breath. Her father had taught her from

an early age that actions held consequences. Now another truth hit her. She realized suddenly that even inaction held consequences.

Maddie took a deep breath and blew it out slow. What she needed was Robert to smooth-talk Trevor. Maybe then he would understand. Maybe then he wouldn't ask so many pointed questions. Unfortunately, Robert was out of town for a few weeks. He'd decided to go to Wyoming Territory and search out a homestead.

Maddie didn't know what to do. She'd always thought when the circumstance arose she would do the right thing, but then Trevor Montgomery had burst into her home looking like the son of the devil all dressed in black, cold rain pouring off him. He'd taken off his hat, turned his silver gaze on her and left her weak in the knees.

In all her life, Maddie had never been weak in the knees. Maybe it was the flu. Yes, and maybe Beth really was in love with her current beau.

Maddie clutched the petition to her chest and took a calming breath. This was all Robert's fault. Her brother had failed to mention that Trevor was a handsome devil. It made her wonder what Evan looked like. Maddie shook off the thought and imagined her disgrace when Trevor discovered the truth. It wouldn't matter that she had repaired the house and kept it nice for his return. Trevor Montgomery didn't look like the understanding sort. She was certain he'd throw her out on her ear.

That would scandalize the ladies in town. She could see Mrs. Albert having some sort of stroke. All the good things she had done in the past would be forgotten when the ladies realized that they had been doped. Why, they would probably sweep their skirts away from her as if she was a woman of scandal.

Then, when her father found out that she had put him through all that for nothing, even her forgiving father wouldn't take her back into her home. She'd be left with the likes of Stuart Bixley.

The thought made her stomach sour.

She did have another alternative—one more palatable, if not less lonely. She could move out to Wyoming Territory with Robert. The thought of miles and miles of empty wilderness was cold comfort. Wilderness or Stuart, the choices were . . . endless.

She thumbed through the letters again. Maybe she didn't have to tell the truth. Maybe Trevor would believe her little charade.

Maybe she was Queen of the fairies.

Madeline sighed. She pushed the box back under her bed and got up. Letters in hand, she squared her shoulders and came to a decision. If Trevor questioned her, she would tell him the truth and take whatever punishment was in store.

If he accepted the story, then she would keep up the pretense. It couldn't hurt. She'd simply move into a small apartment in town. Everyone would accept the appropriateness of her moving out with Trevor home. The ladies may even welcome her into the brigade.

In time she would tell the truth. Her only worry would be if Evan Montgomery showed up before she found the proper opening for her story. A shudder ran through her. She was lucky it was Trevor at the door tonight. It could have been so much worse.

"Maddie, did you find them?" Beth stood in the doorway.

Maddie sent her baby sister a smile. "They're right here," she said and waved the rolled document.

Beth turned toward the kitchen. "She has the petition." Beth's excitement sent prickles of doom down Maddie's back. Maybe she should start packing.

She stepped into the kitchen and braced herself for the impact Trevor had on her senses. He was still handsome. Dark hair fell over his forehead. A day's worth of whiskers shadowed his strong jaw and framed firm lips.

He had the look of a poetic hero right down to the sardonic grin on his handsome mouth. Her knees threatened to buckle and she snagged the back of a nearby chair.

Right now, this moment, Maddie wanted to kill her brother Robert. She hid it behind a gritted smile.

All her life she had gone along with Robert's schemes. They always seemed so clearly thought out. Yet, somehow they never ended well. Even now it had taken two years before the lie caught up with her, but it always caught up with her.

The only good news to the situation was that Amelia was twenty and Beth eighteen. The scandal Maddie was about to create would not affect their chances for marriage.

Trevor stood when she entered the room. It was a gentlemanly thing to do and belayed the suspicion that gleamed from his eyes.

Maddie steeled herself for the accusations to come and crossed the room. She could not keep her hand from trembling as she held out the petition. He glanced from the papers to her face and raised an eyebrow.

"You're trembling."

"I'm not used to being so forcefully accused in my own home." The truth in her statement rang out in the room.

"It's my home too," he said. "There in lies the problem." Trevor took the roll of papers; his hand covered hers briefly. Their gazes clashed and a tingling heat rushed up her arm straight to her heart. She swallowed hard. She'd never experienced that before and was tempted to touch him again to see if it was merely a fluke.

"It was all so terrible," Beth burst in, her conversation breathless, breaking whatever spell the devil wove around Maddie. She sat back down at the table.

Trevor looked away and Maddie put her hands behind her back before she was tempted to do something altogether foolish.

"What was terrible?"

"Why, what father attempted to do," Beth said. She put her elbows on the table, cupped her hands and put her chin in her hands. The action was at once flirtatious and innocent.

"I'm sure Mr. Montgomery is not interested in the story," Maddie said, and forced her wobbly legs to move. She covered her discomfort by clearing the table. To do so, she had to brush past him. He smelled of rain and warm male with a hint of cologne. In short he smelled better than hot chocolate on a cold winter morning.

It was a good thing Robert wasn't in town. She had the sudden urge to throttle him.

Instead, she picked up the dishes and placed them in the sink. Trevor Montgomery was more dangerous to her than a wolf. Like an innocent lamb curious about the wolf, she seemed to want only to touch the danger and savor the taste of it. Maddie pressed the pump on the sink in a poor attempt to distract herself from her doom. Water poured out, laughing and dancing over the few dishes she had to wash.

"I'd love to hear the story," Trevor said and leaned against the end of the counter. His gaze locked on Maddie. "I'm sure it's quite . . . tragic."

"Oh, my," Beth said breathily. "It's like something out of a fairytale. Two years ago father announced to the whole town that Amelia—she's our other sister—and I could not marry unless Maddie married."

"I take it you're the oldest," he said as he continued to ignore the petition in his hand and focus his attention on Maddie.

"Yes," she said, and ignored the odd heat his silver gaze sent to her heart.

"Oh, we all thought that Maddie was too old to marry. After all she was twenty and three at the time. Amelia was eighteen and I was sixteen. Our beaus were horrified of Papa's stipulation. I mean, who would want to marry a spinster of Maddie's age."

The heat of a blush rushed over Maddie's cheeks. Beth made her sound wholly undesirable. Did Trevor think the same thing? Is that what fueled the suspicion she saw in his eyes?

"Indeed, I'm sure a woman of her age is rather set in her ways," Trevor said.

What did he mean by that? Maddie glanced at Trevor and saw a teasing smile cross his lips. It had an odd effect on her knees. She quickly turned back to the dishes.

"My thought exactly," Beth said. "I mean, no one had courted Maddie before, why would they start now?"

"I imagine things seemed rather bleak."

"Oh, I thought I was destined to remain in my father's house forever, but then the oddest thing happened. Suitors seemed to come right out of the woodwork. Why, Maddie had ten or twelve men visiting, but she would have nothing to do with them."

"Really?"

"They weren't interested in marrying me," Maddie said, shook her head at the memory and picked up the tea kettle. She rinsed the dishes with the hot water. "They were interested in the money Beth's suitors were offering to the man who married me."

A grin formed on his devilish face. "It seemed that hopeless?"

The idea still stung Maddie's pride, even after two years. Stiffly she picked up a towel and dried the dishes.

"Of course it was hopeless," Beth interjected. "What no one knew was that Maddie was pining away for your brother Evan. All because of the secret affair they had before your brother left."

"So, you consider it an affair?"

Maddie didn't like the tone of his voice when he said that. "I did not have an affair."

"Maddie was only fifteen at the time," Beth went on to say. "It was all so Romeo and Juliet."

"Except no one died," Trevor added dryly.

"I am not that foolish," Maddie said, and rinsed the last of the dishes.

"The day Evan joined the Army he asked Maddie to wait for him. She said she would, didn't you Maddie?"

It was time to tell the truth. "I—"

"They secretly exchanged promises," Beth pressed on joyfully. "Of course, no one else was present."

"Of course," Trevor said sardonically.

"But a promise is a promise," Beth gushed. "It was so romantic. All those years we thought she simply wasn't interested in anything but her needlework, Maddie was nursing a wounded heart."

"How very . . . loyal of her."

"I think it's all so romantic," Beth said and sighed. She sat up. "Anyway, when Papa made his decree, the whole story came out. One thing led to another, and poof! Maddie ended up here, taking care of your home while she waited patiently for Evan to return."

"How you must pine."

Maddie did not like the way he said that. It was clear he didn't believe any part of the story and she wondered why. Why did the whole town believe her but not Trevor? Did he think that she wasn't good enough for his precious brother? She put the last dish away and turned on him.

"I wonder if you are surprised by the fact that Evan had a fiancée or by the fact that I am the fiancée?" Maddie said. She cocked her head and studied him back. "You sure didn't seem so surprised to find a woman here when you came in, therefore your disbelief must come from the fact that I am the fiancée. Why is that?"

He shook his head. "You're right. When I first rode up I thought that Evan had beaten me home. Then when I saw the pumpkins on the porch, the rag rug as you enter, I figured my brother had wed while I was gone."

"So you aren't shocked by the fact that your brother is

engaged as much as you are shocked that he would be engaged to me." She tried to keep emotion out of her reply, but she still sounded hurt.

"I'm not shocked," he said and frowned at her. "It's just . . ."

"Just what?"

"You don't seem like the kind of girl Evan would bring home."

"I see." Maddie stiffened.

Beth rose quickly. "Maddie is a wonderful cook. She is very neat and has completely restored this house and the barn and gardens. Surely, you can't be disappointed."

"Oh, no," he said softly. "I'm not disappointed with any of the things I've seen."

"See," Beth said and turned to Maddie. "I knew it would all work out." She smiled and patted Trevor on the arm. "Welcome home. I can't wait to tell the ladies one of the Montgomery brothers has finally come home. They'll be thrilled."

"I'm always happy to thrill the ladies," Trevor said, and Maddie believed him.

"Are you going to look at the petitions?" Beth asked.

"I'll examine them later," he said. "I trust they are in order."

"Everything's in order. The mayor himself will vouch for Maddie. Oh, my, look at the time," Beth said when the mantle clock rang out 9 P.M. "I'd better get back before Papa sends our brother Henry out after me." She stood and dipped into a small curtsey. "It was so nice to meet you, Trevor, I mean Mr. Montgomery. You didn't say what I should call you? Is Trevor all right? We are practically family after all."

"I have a feeling you will call me whatever you wish," he said, his sarcasm not lost on Madeline.

"Come on, Beth, I'll see you to the road." Madeline

handed her sister her cloak, grabbed her own shawl, and pushed her sister out the door.

The rain had stopped, but the air was still sharp with a cold chill and the smell of icy rain. Quiet was heavy on the dark air. Maddie's nose and cheeks instantly reddened with the cold.

"Oh, Maddie, he is so handsome, isn't he?" Beth asked as they stepped off the porch. "I had no idea. I bet your Evan is even more beautiful. I am so jealous. Why, if Trevor weren't so much older than me I might fall in love with him." Beth smiled, put her gloves on and hugged Madeline. "Can you imagine if you and I were to marry brothers? Why, we could live side by side. What a hoot that would be."

"Hmm, a hoot," Maddie said. Something inside her balked at the idea of Beth falling in love with Trevor. Beth fell in and out of love every day. Trevor was the sort of complicated man that once you fell for you were lost forever.

"Oh, Maddie, I just had a thought. If Trevor had found his way home, then surely Evan can't be far behind."

Maddie felt a stab of pure horror to her heart. "It's been so long, I really doubt that—"

"But we thought Trevor would never come and here he is. Really, I bet my best bonnet that Evan is on his way home even as we speak. Wouldn't that be wonderful?"

"Wonderful," Maddie parroted. Her body froze in terror.

"Well, I must go," Beth said, oblivious to her sister's plight. She unhooked the reins of her mare.

"You brought the buggy?"

"I was on my way back from town," Beth explained. "There was a poetry reading at the library and with the weather as unpredictable as it is, well, Papa insisted I take the buggy."

Beth stepped up into the covered two-seater. The top swayed with the motion. Beth took the reins firmly and unhooked the brake. "What an exciting evening," Beth gushed. "Why, think of it, Maddie, if Trevor has returned then Evan can't be far behind." Beth let out an exaggerated sigh. "Then you would be in seventh heaven, wouldn't you? Of course you would, and then I would be talking to Papa about a wedding." Beth shook her head, her expression dreamy. "A storybook ending."

"Beth," Maddie said sternly pulling her sister out of her reverie.

"Yes, Maddie?"

"Be careful going home, it's late and the roads are treacherous."

"I'll be fine," Beth said with a little wave. "I can't wait to tell Papa that Trevor has come home and Evan isn't far behind."

"Now, Trevor didn't say a word about Evan coming back."

"He didn't have to, silly. It's how these things happen."

How these things happen.

Maddie swallowed the jolt that just went through her. In one quiet night her whole life was being ripped apart. Where was Robert? Why was he never around when it came time for consequences? Maddie bit her lip, her mind reeling. What would Papa say? What would everyone say about her spending the night in the same house as Trevor Montgomery unchaperoned? "Tell Papa I have a gun and a lock on my door."

Beth laughed then gave a short catchy giggle. "Don't be silly, Maddie. Everyone knows you and Trevor are practically brother and sister." She leaned out and kissed Maddie's cheek. "Go inside, it's cold and you are turning blue."

Maddie frowned and took a step back.

"Go," Beth said, and made a shooing motion with her hand. "I'll be fine and so will you. Just remember, if Trevor came home, then Evan can come home." Beth sent her a beatific smile. "I bet you can't wait."

"Good night, Beth."

"Good night."

Maddie watched her sister drive off. Then she turned reluctantly back toward the house. She had to go in some-time. It would be too suspicious if she slept in the barn.

Chapter Four

T revor frowned at the cozy fire that popped and snapped in the parlor hearth. Well, heck, he thought, this certainly was not the homecoming he expected. He eased his way over to the fire, taking note of the care that was taken with his mother's things. If nothing else, the little usurper had kept the place from ruin and neglect.

The cabin was indeed well cared for. The curtains were clean and starchly pressed. The windows washed with obvious pride. The woodwork smelled of lemon oil, even the floor shone.

He reached up and ran his fingers along a row of his mother's favorite volumes. It was clear that Madeline loved books. These were perfectly preserved. Their covers clean, their pages only slightly worn. His mother's rocking chair sat in front of the fire; a pretty piece of needlework sat on the seat.

He ignored the dull pain that radiated through his body, and ran his fingers along the smooth worn arms of the chair. A different kind of pain went through him; memories of his mother sitting in this chair, mending or reading.

He looked up and fought back the wave of grief that bolted through him. It would have been better to find the place in ruins. Now, like this, it was too familiar. It brought back too many memories of the things that were lost to him forever.

The door opened, letting in a blast of icy air. It smelled of danger and darkness with just a hint of rose water. He glanced over to see her standing in the doorway studying him.

"You might as well come in and close the door," he said. "I don't think I have the heart to attack you."

Grimly she did as he ordered. "I have the guns, remember?"

He chuckled then. It was a rusty sound, one that surprised even him. "You've done a good job with the house," he said evenly. He was tired and his bones ached. The beautiful woman in the kitchen watched him warily.

He knew he should leave, at the very least he should sleep in the barn with his horse. Then in the morning, he should go into town and find a room.

Surrounded by his mother's things, she did strange things to his worn out heart. He couldn't bring himself to leave.

He couldn't accept that she belonged to his brother and yet, the alternative was worse.

Finally, she shook out her shawl and hung it on the back of a chair. Then she turned to face him as a man might face an executioner. "I will pack my things and leave in the morning."

"Why?" he asked.

She blinked, her expression one of confusion and uncertainty. "This home is rightfully yours."

Trevor straightened away from the fireplace. He wasn't going to let her go that easily. If what she said was the truth, then he wouldn't be the one to throw his brother's love out on the street.

"If promises were given," he said, "I won't be the one to come between you and Evan."

Fear and disbelief flashed over her beautiful face. "Surely, I can't stay here if you are here?"

"Why not?" Trevor asked. "From the sounds of things everyone believes you are practically my sister. The last thing I want to do is throw you out on the street."

"I have money of my own. I can move into town."

"I don't think so," he said. "In fact, I must insist that you stay. I wouldn't want Evan thinking that I was the one who drove you away."

"Have you heard from Evan?" she asked, her voice aquiver. Was it telling that she hugged her elbows until her knuckles were white?

Trevor couldn't tell if she was afraid he had or hadn't heard from his brother. "Not since before our mother's death."

"He didn't come for the funeral."

"Neither did you."

She flinched ever so slightly at the accusation in his tone, and then raised her chin. "Your mother didn't know me," she said. "Without Evan there, there was no reason for me to attend the funeral."

Trevor blew out a breath. He was being a terrible house-guest and yet he couldn't bring himself to stop. Somehow it angered him that she belonged to Evan. It was hard enough to come home. Harder still to find an angel there who was out of reach. "You're right," he said. "I'm sorry for badgering you. Truce?"

She relaxed slightly. "Truce." Then she took a deep breath and blew it out slowly. "I'm sorry, if I seem defensive. You were just so . . . unexpected."

He lifted the corner of his mouth in a wry smile. "I'm told that a lot."

"I will make up the bed in the second bedroom for you. Unless you wish to have the one I'm currently in. Then it will be a few minutes before I can move my things."

He waved the notion away. "The other bedroom was always mine. I'm used to the bed."

"Then I'll make it right up."

"I didn't expect to find anyone in the house," he said. "It's enough that you shared your supper with me. I can make up my own bed."

She stood near the table obviously reluctant to come any closer. She clutched the edges of her robe together near her throat. "I had no intention of stealing your home from you," she said. "It had been neglected for two years when I moved in here."

"I suppose there is such a thing as squatter's rights," he said, unhappy with himself for not coming home sooner. "Legal papers or not, there are some who believe that possession is nine-tenths of the law." He moved closer to her, stalking her, testing her reaction. It was somewhere between bewilderment and attraction. She kept her chin up and her stance firm.

Her reaction egged him on and he moved in closer.

"I told you I will move out tomorrow," she said. Her tone was brave and defiant.

"No." The word came out as a direct order. An ex-military colonel, Trevor was used to being obeyed when he used that tone of voice. "From what your sister says the whole town thinks you belong here. I won't have them thinking I was so cruel as to throw you to the wolves." *Unless, of course, you are a wolf yourself, bent on stealing my family home.*

He watched her carefully to see her reaction. Instead of guilt, his comment angered her. Her shoulders squared and her chin went up. She reached for the chair behind her but remained firm as he approached. "Why do you care what the town thinks? You've been gone for nearly ten years."

He took a deep breath and blew it out slow, easing his way toward her. "This is my home, Madeline. I've left it long enough."

"So, then you are home to stay?"

"Yes," he said, and crowded her against the table. He noted her reaction to him. Her hands trembled. A flush covered her cheeks and annoyance flashed through her gaze. "Does that upset your plans?" His words were a whisper against her cheek.

"Hardly," she said between gritted teeth. She moved away from him, putting the pine table between them. "My only goal in life is to live it unmolested by another."

He laughed, then offered a full belly laugh. "Honey, if you truly had an affair with my brother, then I highly doubt you are unmolested."

Her gaze flashed fire and brimstone. He swore she thought about reaching for her rifle. He cocked an eyebrow at her, daring her to deny it. If she did, then it was certain she had made up the entire tale. If she didn't then . . . well, either way she was hardly the innocent she portrayed.

That thought made his heart heavy and his soul increasingly tired. He backed away. "Forgive me. It has been a long cold journey and exhaustion has caused me to be boorishly rude." All of a sudden his strange attraction to her was replaced with an odd ache in his joints and a pounding headache.

"Perhaps it would be best if we were to discuss the situation in the morning," she said.

"Yes, of course."

She had a point. He needed the night to rest his aching body and think things through. "So, for now, let's retreat to our prospective corners," he suggested. "I'll even be so good as to leave the guns with you."

"I wouldn't have it any other way," she said, and picked up the rifle and his holster off the cabinet. "A girl can't be too careful these days."

"No, I don't suppose she can."

"There are clean sheets in the chest at the foot of the bed. The towel near the basin is fresh this morning. Should you need anything further, I would advise you to knock on my door. I am a light sleeper and I know full well how to shoot this rifle with some accuracy."

He smiled at her boast. "I suppose your brother Robert taught you how to shoot."

"Yes," she said and stepped toward the bedroom door opposite the kitchen from his. "He also taught me to keep a lock on my bedroom door. After all, you never know what might attempt to enter your room while you sleep."

"A fine idea," he countered. "I'll be sure and lock mine as well. I wouldn't want anyone to be tempted to seduce me in my sleep."

She gasped. "I would never."

"Would you not?" He raised an eyebrow. "You've been a woman without a man too long."

"If I needed a man it surely wouldn't be you."

"Oh, yes, that's right. You're saving yourself for my little brother."

"You overstep the bounds of decency," she said, her color high. "I will excuse it as you have told me more than once that you are tired. Good night, sir."

Affronted, she turned on her heel and stepped into her bedroom slamming the door behind her. He waited, listening until he heard the final click of the lock, then the sound of a chair being dragged to the front of the door for good measure.

He moved tiredly to his room and shook his head. Madeline was a contradiction. Certainly a mystery he intended to solve. Her spirit and beauty were far superior to any he'd ever seen in all of his travels. He wondered how she had become involved with Evan.

Evan. Trevor wondered if his handsome, charming brother had any idea this willful beauty waited for him. If Trevor had found her first, he would not have stayed away so very long.

Pain radiated around his heart. Pain at the loss of his

dreams. Pain at the realization that even here he didn't quite belong.

He turned into the dark room. A lamp sat on the top of an empty bureau. He lit the lamp and surveyed the area. His old bed still rested under the window, a sturdy trunk at its feet. Inside the trunk were sheets that smelled of care and sunshine. Sheets that his mother had sewn when she was young and strong and happy.

He sat on the bed and buried his face in them. Memories of happier times assailed him and he knew one thing for certain. No matter what Madeline's motives had been, she had done him a favor. Like it or not, all the things that blinded him with memories and pain would have been lost had she not rescued them from neglect. Oddly, he found he needed them now more than ever. He got up and made the bed. Then he pulled off his shirt and socks. The floor was cold, but oddly enough he liked it. His head pounded and the room was unusually warm. He slipped into the cool sheets and closed his eyes. Tomorrow, he would be a gentleman and move into town until he could get to the truth behind her appearance, but for tonight he needed this house, this bed and these memories.

Maddie pulled the top sheet and quilt up around her neck. Her whole being hummed and she doubted she would get a wink of sleep. The insufferable man was at once insulting and forgiving. Guilt and uncertainty filled her. The right thing to do was to pack her things. She couldn't stay in his house. She had no real claim to it.

On the other hand, he was right. The ladies would despise him if they thought he had anything to do with her return home. The only thing to do would be for her to confess her ruse in front of her father and the whole town.

Only then would the blame fall where it should, square on her shoulders. She sighed and turned on her side. It was an admission she wasn't looking forward to. Maybe she could simply leave town. She had a spinster aunt who lived in Ohio. Maddie sat up with a sigh. Ohio wasn't the answer either. She had lied, and for two years it had been easy. She shook her head. "What a wicked web we weave when first we practice to deceive."

She stared at the door, her imagination working overtime. Trevor Montgomery had a strange effect on her. His very presence made her heart speed up and her hands tremble. When he had spoken of ravishment she thought her knees would turn to water.

When he had crowded her near the table, she had been horrified and excited at the same time. What was wrong with her? She never felt that way about a man before. It was almost as if she had come alive the moment he'd stepped into her kitchen.

Maddie puzzled over that thought for a moment. Was this how sleeping beauty felt when she was awakened by the prince's kiss? Maddie shook off the fanciful thought. The man was insufferable and contradictory. If he ever dared to kiss her, he would surely cry out to the world that it was she who was seducing him.

Maddie realized she should be counting her blessings. It could have been Evan who showed up unannounced. Then she would be in a real pickle.

She got up and looked out her window. The rain was back. It drizzled cold and icy, filling the inky darkness with the sound of water on the roof.

Her mind reeled over Beth's comments. With Trevor back, Evan would be sure to follow. Soon. There was nothing for it. She had to face the truth. She had to tell everyone that she had duped them. That the romance they smiled about, the deep-seated love they all admired, had been nothing but a horrible lie meant to deceive them.

Maddie's stomach ached. She hugged herself close. She didn't have many friends, but the ladies of the town had rallied around the romantic story. What would they do when they learned they had been conned? Mrs. Selis and Mrs. Lance had gone out of their way to champion her story. Crossing them would be the same thing as societal suicide.

Still, there was no alternative. Trevor Montgomery had returned and his brother was sure to follow.

The quiet sound of rain was smashed by a horrible crashing sound from the next room. Maddie's senses went on full alert. "Mr. Montgomery?" she called and reached for her rifle. The sound of cups falling and a loud thud answered her call.

Heart pounding, she cocked the hammer back and called again. "Trevor? Are you all right?"

A groan answered her. Whoever was in the kitchen was in distress. Earlier, she had put a heavy chair in front of her door. She didn't know if she had done it to keep him out or herself inside. Now she pulled the chair away and called again. "Trevor?"

Silence replied cold and dangerous. Rifle in hand, she unlocked her door and peered out. The kitchen was dark, lit only by the tiny pool of lamplight coming from Trevor's open bedroom door. The kitchen door was still secure, so unless someone had crawled in through a window, the only person in the kitchen should be Trevor Montgomery. She stepped out. The smooth wooden floor was cold on her bare feet. "Trevor?" Uncertainty made the word come out closer to a whisper.

A groan answered her. Her eyes adjusted to the half-light and she saw him. He lay face down on the kitchen floor. A chair was knocked over and a ceramic mug in pieces rested near his hand.

Maddie put down the rifle and rushed to his side. A dark substance pooled near his head. Horror washed over her. One touch and she had an idea of what had happened. The substance was water. Trevor must have come into the kitchen looking for water because he was burning up with a high fever. "Mr. Montgomery . . . Trevor. Are you okay?"

He muttered something dark and horrible. She stood up quickly, more afraid than she had ever been in her life. She wrapped her arms around her waist and stared. He shivered on the cold floor and groaned again.

"Get a hold of yourself, Madeline Morgan," she chided herself out loud. "The man is clearly sick and needs your help." The first thing she needed to do was get him back in the bed. Trevor was huge. His well-muscled torso bare, he wore only the pants he had had on earlier. She shook his shoulder. His skin was much too warm on her palm. "Trevor, Trevor can you hear me?"

"I hear you," he said through chattering teeth.

"You need to get up."

"What?"

"You're burning up with fever and it isn't good for you to be on the floor."

"It's so hot in here. Why do you keep the fire so high?" he demanded, and curled into a ball.

She glanced at the fireplace. The fire was banked, only red coals glowed. "Get up. It's not the fire," she said. "It's fever."

"The floor feels good."

"You have to get into bed. Can you sit up?"

He pushed her away. Maddie bit her bottom lip and tried again. "Please, you have to get up." She pulled his arm until she managed to get him to sit up.

"What are you doing, woman?" he demanded, and tried to bat her away. "Leave me alone. I told you not to seduce me."

She stood and put her hands on her hips. "The last thing I want to do at this moment is seduce you."

He put his head in his hands. "What did you hit me with?" he said in a jagged whisper.

"I didn't touch you," she replied. "You must have fallen

over a chair. I heard the crash and came out to find you face down on the floor."

"It's so darn hot in here."

"It's fever," she said and hunkered down beside him. "Can you get up? I can help you back to bed, but I can't carry you."

He shivered hard and she grabbed her shawl off the peg by the door and draped it over his bare shoulders. "You have to get up," she said with as much authority as she could muster. She put his arm around her shoulder and pushed him up.

He was heavy, almost too heavy for her to bear. "Come on," she said. "March soldier!"

"Too darn tired to march," he muttered, his head rolled onto her shoulder. "You smell good."

"Thank you. But we need to concentrate on getting you back into bed."

"It's cold. When did it get so cold?"

He radiated so much heat that she broke out in a sweat. It was clear she wasn't going to get him across the kitchen. Her bed was closer. It was an easy decision. She wasn't sleeping anyway. "Come on," she said and gritted her teeth under his weight. "Just a few feet and we'll get you in bed."

He groaned, but moved when she did. After what seemed like forever, she finally got him to the bed. He sat down on the edge and cradled his head. "Someone split my head open," he said.

"Lay back," she ordered and pushed on his shoulder. He did as he was told, his handsome head landing unceremoniously on her pillow. She tried not to think about how intimate the situation was. Instead, she pulled her quilt up around his shoulders just as his teeth began to chatter.

"It's so blasted cold. Now I remember why I didn't come back. Winters are hard in Wisconsin," he said through chattering teeth.

Maddie raced through the house and tore the blankets off

his bed. She rushed through the kitchen again, wincing when her bare foot stood on a slice of broken ceramic. She hobbled toward the bed and tucked a second and third blanket on him. He reached up and grabbed her wrist. "Water please, miss," he begged. "I'd give anything for a drink of water."

"Stay under the covers," she ordered. She tucked him back in and tiptoed out into the kitchen. This time, she was careful to avoid the broken pottery. She filled a pitcher with water and grabbed a tin cup. She worked her way back to her bedroom, and lit a hurricane lamp. Then she poured water into the cup and offered it to him.

He drank like a man who had just traveled through the desert. "Thank you," he whispered when he had finished. "God bless you."

Maddie's heart went out to the handsome devil. From the way he asked for water, it was clear he'd fought fever during the war. She wondered what it must have been like to beg for water in the middle of a war-ravished camp or worse. What if he had fought a fever with shrapnel in him, festering with infection? The men who had returned from the war had never spoken of the hardships, but Maddie was well read. She had absorbed every horrifying word regarding the condition of the field hospitals. "Rest, now," she said softly. "I'm here."

"Thank goodness for angels," he muttered and closed his eyes.

Maddie stared down at his handsome face. She knew she was far from an angel. Still, the idea that he would find her one soothed her troubled heart.

She went back into the kitchen and opened a cabinet. Inside she kept her elixirs and tonics for just such emergencies. She pulled down a bottle and found a spoon. Then she tiptoed back into her room, and climbed onto the bed beside him. It was the only way she would be able to leverage him into a position where he could take the medicine.

She put her arm around his head and lifted him by his shoulders.

"Still trying to seduce me, darling?" he asked, his voice husky. It made the hairs on her skin stand up on end, and heat pool inside her.

"You need to take some medicine," she said as sharply as possible. Someone had to remain all business. She poured the elixir into the spoon and held it in front of his mouth. "Take it," she ordered.

He opened wide and she shoved the liquid in. He swallowed then spit and sputtered. "Are you trying to poison me?" he gasped.

"Wouldn't that be convenient?" She lowered his head back down on her pillow. "Sleep. It'll be dawn in a few hours and I will be able to go get the doctor."

"Don't need a doctor," he groused and snuggled into the blankets. "I got me an angel."

She stood and stared down at him. His thick black hair rested on the pillowcase, making him look like a small mischievous boy. Her heart melted at the sight. "Make up your mind," she whispered. "Am I an angel or a devil?"

He didn't answer. He was fast asleep. She sighed and realized that she needed to bandage her foot and clean up the kitchen. Okay, so packing was out of the question. She couldn't leave until he was well.

She limped into the kitchen. It was just as well. This small farmhouse had been her sanctuary for two years. She wasn't quite ready to give it up.

Chapter Five

"It looks like malaria," Doc Emerson said as he closed up his medical bag. "Probably a re-occurrence. It happens sometimes. He was lucky he made it home."

"I appreciate your coming out so early," Maddie said. "His fever ran so high last night I was worried that he would not come out of it."

"He's a strong man. Had a set of lungs on him from the day he was born. I should know, I delivered him." Doc smiled at her and put his hat on his head. "See that he gets plenty of fluids. Keep the room warm and cool cloths on his forehead. I'll write a prescription and have your brother Henry bring it by as soon as the pharmacist fills it. I'll be back in a few days to check on him."

"Thank you," Maddie said and escorted the doctor to the door.

"And Maddie," the doctor said and turned toward her.

"Yes?"

"Once that fever breaks he's going to be weak for a while." Doc looked her square in the eye. "It's a good thing he has you."

"I'm going to move into town," she said, panic rising in

her throat. "So, please let everyone know that I'm not staying."

"He's part of your family now, Maddie," Doc said with a sincere look. "He's been through a lot, what with the war, his mother's death and now this. He'll need someone strong to look out for him until he can get back on his feet."

"Mrs. Allison can come nurse him."

"Mrs. Allison isn't family," Doc said. "Keep in mind that he's housed you for two years. The least you can do is stay by his side until he doesn't need you."

Maddie pressed her lips together. She had the distinct feeling that Doc Emerson surmised the truth. If that were so, how many other people knew that she had lied about her engagement?

"You're a good girl, Maddie," he said and patted her arm. "You'll do the right thing."

Maddie watched him get up into his carriage and canter off. The rain had left with the morning sun. The air had been scrubbed clean, the sky blue above the browns, yellows and reds of the changing leaves. It was her favorite time of year. The farmstead was beautiful in the circle of glorious trees, and the larder fat with the fall harvest.

If Trevor hadn't arrived last night, she would have spent the day taking care of the animals, chopping wood for her winter stockpile, and reading in the soft warm sunlight. She went out to her woodpile and gathered some of the more seasoned logs.

She sighed. She really did love the place. It would be hard to leave, and Doc was right. She owed Trevor for the privilege of living here.

Still she also owed the townspeople an explanation and an apology. The thought of the looks of horror and disappointment on the ladies' faces nearly killed her. She bit her lip. Putting off telling the truth is what had gotten her in this mess. It would just get worse the longer she waited and, yet, if she told the truth now there would be no one to help Trevor.

She supposed waiting just a few more days couldn't possibly make things any worse. Unless, of course, Beth was right and Evan showed up. Maddie shuddered at the thought. Surely fate would not be so cruel.

She glanced at her bedroom window. Trevor Montgomery lay in her bed weak as a kitten. She had no choice but to tempt fate and stay to nurse him. She would not abandon him in his time of need. It was purely coincidence that his illness put off her revealing the truth.

For better or for worse, Maddie made up her mind. She'd stay until Trevor no longer needed her. When Henry came out with the prescription, she'd ask him to stay and cut a cord. She would need the extra fuel to keep the fire going until Trevor was well enough to cut his own.

Then she'd move into town, but not before she told him the truth. Once she faced Trevor, she would face the town and take her knocks. In a way it would be a relief. She was a strong believer in consequences. It would be good to get them over with.

She entered the house, closed the door behind her and dumped the wood in the metal holder by the fireplace. She quickly took off her gloves and poked the fire with the iron. The clock on the mantle told her it was time to check on Trevor. With any luck, his fever will break today.

He was in the enemy's camp and they delighted in torturing him. Trevor gritted his chattering teeth and fought against the urge to cry out. First they overheated him, and then they'd throw him out into the snow until his fingers were numb. Then back to the flames of hell.

He remembered this torture. He'd been here before. This time was different though. This time an angel appeared, bringing him water whenever he thought to call for it.

When the cold got unbearable, she would come and wrap him in her wings and warm him.

"I know they sent you," he told the angel.

"Who sent me?"

"The enemy," he said, and took a sip of water. It tasted finer than the finest wine. He swallowed greedily. "Thank you."

She moved away. He didn't want her to go. He needed her to understand. So he grabbed her wrist. It was oddly delicate in his hand; the skin soft and a strong pulse fluttered under his fingers. "Funny, I never thought about angels having a heartbeat."

"Let go of me," she said. Her voice was music to his ears. He did as she asked.

"Don't go," he said. The strength to convey his desire quickly faded.

"I'm not leaving."

"Good." He patted the bed beside him. "Please sit with me a while and tell me what it's like."

She sat beside him. Her scent soothed his senses. She smelled like rosewater and cinnamon. "Tell you what what is like?"

He put his head down on the pillow and the cold receded. "What heaven is like. Is my brother there?"

"Evan?"

"Yes," he said and closed his eyes. "Did Evan make it to heaven?"

"Is Evan dead?"

"I don't know. Don't you know?"

"Shh," the angel said. "Don't worry over it."

"Did Evan miss heaven?"

She put a cool cloth on his forehead. It felt so sweet and soothing. He let out a sigh of satisfaction. He put his hand on her hand. The texture of her skin was a comfort in the madness. "Did he?"

"Heaven's a pretty big place. I think it would be easy for an angel not to know every single person."

"Oh." He felt himself slipping away. "Promise me something, darling."

"What?"

"Promise me that no matter how big heaven is, you'll find me."

"Shh. It's okay. You're going to be fine."

"Promise me you won't lose me."

"I promise."

Satisfied, Trevor let the darkness draw him back.

It seemed the whole town was excited to have Trevor back. Several people had stopped by for a visit. Maddie had had to post a note that Trevor was currently under the weather, but would be happy to visit with everyone once he was feeling better.

The people would smile and nod at her with encouraging looks. It was disturbing. They wanted to encourage her to remain hopeful. Now that Trevor was home they all expected Evan at any moment. A shudder went down Maddie's spine. If she didn't know better they were planning a June wedding. Disaster loomed on the horizon and she couldn't run from it. Doc Emerson was right. She needed to stay at least until Trevor was able to get around on his own.

Perhaps the best thing to do right now was to remain at home. Out of the public eye. Speculation drove her nuts. What she really wanted was to tell the truth and take her medicine, but she couldn't do it. Not yet. Not while Trevor needed her.

If the town knew the truth they would frown on an unattached girl caring for a sick bachelor. Trevor would be left to the mercy of the matrons in town.

Maddie stared down at the book on her lap. It was Charles Dickens' *Tale of Two Cities*. The books would have to stay with the house. She rubbed the treasured pages and glanced at Trevor. Maybe he would let her take a few volumes.

She sighed. What was she thinking? They were his mother's books. Once he found out that she had lied her way into his home she'd never see these books again.

She got up and checked his forehead. It was still very warm. The fever had not broken in three days. She'd asked Doc to come back out this morning, but he simply shook his head and told her that Trevor had to ride out the fever. It was typical for it to last ten days.

That meant she had seven days to enjoy this lovely home and the beautiful library. Then her world would come crashing down.

Trevor reached out and grabbed her wrist. "Stay," he said through dry lips. She allowed him to pull her onto the bed beside him. He'd had a few spells where he'd hallucinated and always, he'd drawn her close.

If she were to be truthful with herself, she knew she liked these short encounters. He was weak with fever and yet his grip was strong. They'd talked about Evan and about his childhood. He'd revealed things that she knew a man would never tell a soul. Yet, he told her because he believed her to be an angel.

"Do you want me to get you some water?"

"No. Please, just stay with me."

She made herself comfortable on the bed beside him. He put his head in her lap. She ran her fingers absently through his thick black hair. It felt soft and cool next to his heated skin. "My mother used to do that whenever I was sick."

"Do what?"

"Brush her fingers through my hair," he said, and threw his arm over her thighs.

Maddie swallowed at the intimacy of the situation. She reasoned that it really didn't mean anything. The man was crazy with fever. It was her job to see that he was comfortable. She continued to run her fingers absently through his hair. She was surprised to find that it soothed her as well. "Trevor?"

"Yes?"

"Where have you been since the war? It's been years. Why didn't you come home?"

"Nothing here for me."

Something in her heart squeezed. He was a very handsome man. Why didn't he have a love waiting for him? "Did you never fall in love?"

"Too angry," he said, his eyes still closed. His hands tightened on her skirt. He had handsome hands. Blocky yet strong, they were hands that spoke volumes. It was clear that they were hands that protected what was his. At the same time, their strength gave way to a controlled gentleness whenever they stroked her skirts. Did his hands never stoke a woman with love?

The very thought kicked her pulse into high gear. She cleared her throat. "Why were you angry?"

"Too many reasons."

"Are you still angry?"

"No." He blew out a breath and snuggled into her lap. "Now, I'm tired, too tired to fight any more."

"So you came home."

"I hurt. Thought maybe home would fix that."

Like a wounded animal he'd come home. She reached for the water pitcher and told herself that Trevor Montgomery was a man, no more, no less. But that didn't explain away her strange attraction or the simple melting of her heart when he talked about his family and about his home. "Here, drink this."

"Medicine?" he asked with a grimace.

"Water." He rose up, opened his silver eyes and gazed at her. It was clear that his gaze was clouded with fever and yet he seemed to see into her soul. As if he knew the strange emotions he elicited inside her. As if he knew how truly lonely she was.

He took a long sip from the cup and handed it back to her. "Thank you." He settled away from her. She tucked the blankets in around him.

"You're welcome."

"You can't be my brother's fiancée."

Something akin to fear rushed along her skin. "Why?"

"Evan would never fall for an angel."

Relief followed. He still thought she was the angel he talked to in his dreams. "Rest," she said, and got off the bed.

He reached out for her. "Don't leave me, darling."

"I won't, I promise." She got up and put the water cup back near the pitcher.

"Madeline." Her name was somehow different when he spoke it. She turned to see that his eyes were clear as they gazed at her.

"Yes?"

"I'm sorry."

She swallowed her apprehension. "I beg your pardon?"

"I'm sorry it took me so long to come home to you."

"Hush now," she said. "Get some rest." He closed his eyes and she retreated to the relative safety of the kitchen. She leaned against the counter for support. It was the fever talking of course. A man as beautiful and dangerous as Trevor Montgomery would never look at her twice. She wrapped her arms around her waist and hugged herself. For the first time in her life she found herself wishing that wasn't true.

The mantle clock chimed out the time. It was nine o'clock in the evening of the tenth day that Trevor had been with her. Maddie sat in the living room mending the few clothes that he brought home with him. It was clear they once were finely tailored, but that was a few years back.

They hadn't been repaired, which was too bad. The material was lovely. She fingered the wool worsted on the third pair of pants. That first morning, she had found Trevor's saddlebags in the stable along with a fine horse. It took three days before she unpacked the bags and found two pairs of slacks, two shirts and three pairs of socks. A well-worn uniform was wrapped up in his saddle blanket, a well-preserved memento of his life.

A fine fire popped and crackled in the hearth. Outside the windows was the darkness of fall and the surrounding woods. A slight breeze blew, shaking the trees and causing shadows to press against the glass.

Trevor's fever had broken in the middle of the night and now he slept. She sat in her favorite of the Montgomery chairs and rocked. It was a handcrafted oak rocker that cradled her body. She tried not to think about how soon she would lose this cozy house and these lovely amenities; how soon she would have to stand in front of the entire town and admit what she had done.

"Why am I sleeping in your bed?"

Startled, Maddie looked up to see Trevor leaning against the doorframe. He stood dressed only in slacks, his chest and feet bare. He looked exhausted from his efforts.

"What are you doing out of bed?" Maddie asked and jumped up to help him.

"I went to sleep in my bed and woke up in yours," he said, his tone suspicious. "Why?"

"I seduced you," Maddie quipped. She couldn't help herself. His question was so absurd. "Don't you remember?"

He cocked a dark eyebrow at her, his gaze clear and seeing way too much. "Really?"

"Of course not," she said and took his arm. She put it over her shoulders and encouraged him to lean on her while she took him back to bed. "You have been sick with fever for almost ten days. You need to go back to bed."

"I suppose you nursed me all by yourself."

"Nonsense, Doctor Emerson was here several times. He said it was malaria, probably a re-occurrence."

Trevor frowned. His handsome face was so close. She was suddenly aware of the strength in the arm that was draped around her shoulders. Even weak he was stronger than she ever dreamed of being. "I thought I outran that."

She pushed him onto the bed, pulled back the covers and waited. He stuck his legs under and allowed her to tuck him back in. "Obviously you didn't. Can I get you something? I have some soup on the stove and there's a pitcher of fresh water on the nightstand."

He reached out and grabbed her wrist. It was something she was getting used to. "You didn't tell me why I'm in your bed and not mine."

"You must have gotten up to get water. I heard a crash and came out to find you passed out on the kitchen floor. You were burning up with fever. This room was closer."

"So you carried me in here?" He sounded skeptical.

"You walked," she said and put her hands on her hips. "I might be big for a woman, but I'm not that strong."

"What do you mean, you're big for a woman? You only come up under my shoulder."

"That's because you, sir, are exceedingly tall."

"Hmm." He put his head down on the pillow and closed his eyes. "Good night, Miss Madeline," he said. Then he was fast asleep.

Maddie looked down at him. How could a man who looked so sweet while he slept be so dangerous when he was awake? Maddie tucked him in and left the room. She remembered Beth's reaction to Trevor. She flirted and talked as if she didn't see the dangerous man beneath the sardonic smile. Maddie glanced at her reflection in the black window. Or maybe Trevor was only dangerous to her.

* * *

Trevor felt as if he'd rammed himself into a mountain and fell a few hundred feet. Every part of him hurt, but he knew from experience that he had to get up and get around. It was the only thing that helped him gain strength. Right now he was as weak as a newborn kitten.

The house was oddly quiet as he padded through the kitchen. A glance outside the kitchen window told him that Madeline was doing laundry. That's how Trevor knew it was Monday. He leaned against the counter and watched her.

She was dressed in a simple blouse and skirt. The hoops of her skirt were minimized. Her sleeves were rolled up. The linen of her blouse moved with her, hugging and concealing her curves. She brushed a long, loose hair out of her face and put a basket of wet clothing down.

Then she gathered up clothes pins in her apron pocket, picked up a sheet out of the basket, folded it in half and pinned it to the line that was strung between two poles his father had set many years ago.

Watching her work with grace and quiet efficiency made him homesick for family. This was his family home, but his family was long gone. The only one who remained was this mysterious woman who called herself his brother's fiancée.

He shouldn't be looking at her with such need. Trevor blew out a long breath and scrubbed his hands over his face. His beard was ten days old and itchy. A bath and a shave would go a long way toward helping him shake the strange emotions that filled him whenever he saw Madeline.

Normally, he'd go into town and get a bath and a shave at the barbershop, but he was too weak. Besides, he doubted Madeline would let him. She took her job as caregiver a bit too seriously. He grinned at the memory of how she just assumed he needed her help to get back into bed last night. He had let her put his arm around her.

She smelled sweet and appealing. She had been soft and compelling. It had been a long time since he'd been cared for and he found he liked it. He had to be careful. She wasn't his to want. She belonged to his ever-charming brother Evan.

Trevor shook off the envy that came over him at the thought. His gaze went back to the woman hanging up the laundry. What would it have been like if Madeline had been waiting for him to come home from the war? If he'd had a beautiful, intelligent woman waiting for him, he would have been home the day after his regiment was released. So, where was Evan? What had kept him from their mother's funeral and this woman's heart?

Suspicion washed over him. None of this made any sense. Evan wasn't the kind to fall in love. He wasn't the kind to appreciate the strength and beauty of an intelligent woman. So, what then was Madeline Morgan doing at his family homestead?

Madeline opened the door and smiled. The fresh sweet scent of fall blew in with her. The impact on Trevor's soul was nearly too much to bear. He leaned heavily on the counter and tried to concentrate on his suspicions.

"What are you doing up?" she asked, her voice filled with concern. She closed the door quickly and put down the basket. "You should be in bed."

"I'm done with the bed," he replied, suddenly grumpy with the whole situation.

"Doctor Emerson said you had to stay in bed for a few days or you might have a relapse." She moved toward him as if to marshal him back into the bedroom.

"No." He put his hand up to ward her off. She stopped short and blinked. He softened his tone. "I've been through this before. The longer I stay in bed the worse it is."

Puzzled, she asked. "Are you sure?"

"Yes."

"Oh." She twisted her hands in her apron and glanced

about as if looking for something to say. It was a charming, awkward moment. One a trespasser wouldn't have. He decided to rescue her.

"I was looking for the hipbath." He ran his hand over his rough beard. "I think a bath and a shave will help me feel better."

"Yes, of course," she brightened. "The bath is in the lean-to. I'll be happy to heat up some water and draw it for you." She paused. "I don't have anything for you to use to shave."

"There's a small kit in my saddlebags," he said. "I'll go get it while you draw the bath."

She blushed a very becoming shade of red, drawing his attention and feeding his doubts. "I brought your saddlebags in while you were sick. I thought you might have a prescription or something in them."

He raised an eyebrow. She stammered on, charmingly embarrassed about going through his things. It was clear that, at least in this matter, she wasn't lying.

"I found your clothes. They weren't in the best condition, so I took the liberty of washing, ironing and mending them. They're hanging in the wardrobe in the bedroom you're sleeping in."

"I see."

"I put your saddlebags in the wardrobe as well. So your shave kit should be in there." She pointed to the bedroom. "I'll get started on drawing your bath."

She escaped back out the front door. Trevor shook his head. Everything about her seemed genuine and yet he knew in his heart of hearts that even if Evan had courted her, he would not have fallen in love with her. Evan didn't know how to love anyone but himself.

Trevor frowned at the dichotomy. Who was Madeline Morgan? The question itched at his brain like a bad rash. If he didn't ache so bad, he'd be better able to work out the mystery.

He heard a sudden thump and large bump. He realized it was the sound of Maddie struggling with the bath. He remembered that the lean-to was a small storage room his father had built off the kitchen. If she were to bring the hipbath into the kitchen, she'd have to drag the thing out of the lean-to, over the porch and through the kitchen door. The hipbath was made of tin so it wasn't heavy, but it was bulky.

If she were to draw his bath, she would need his help. He might be in a weakened state, but he could still help. He followed her out the door. The lean-to door was open, inviting him into the darkness. It was cool and held the musty scent of bare dirt combined with onion, herbs and smoked meats hanging from the rafters. His eyes adjusted on the barrels of potatoes and other tubers. Stocks of produce preserved to help feed them through the winter.

It was a storehouse as rich as any he'd ever seen. It was clear that she had put a lot of work into it.

"I've never seen it this grand."

She gasped and straightened, obviously startled by his appearance at the door. "You scared me," she accused.

"I didn't mean to," he said and moved farther into the small lean-to. The space was cramped with the treasure she had stored there. He stopped a half-inch from her. Her beautiful gaze watched him warily. In the dark cool room, there was only her. He reached up and brushed her wayward hair behind her ear. She smelled of sunshine and laundry. Her hair was cool and silky, her skin soft. He couldn't help himself. He brushed his hand along her cheek. Her eyes widened and she inhaled, bringing his attention to her lovely bosom, then back to her sweet full lips.

The air between them warmed considerable. It took all of the strength he had not to bend down and kiss her startled mouth.

He couldn't. She was not his and worse, he couldn't even be sure she was who she said she was. He might be weak from fever, but he wasn't stupid. Attractive or no, he had to take a step back.

"I thought you might need some help." He shoved his hands in his pockets. "I heard you banging things around and, if I remember right, the tub is bulky."

She blinked and he swore she looked disappointed. She hid it by bustling around and putting the hipbath between them. "I've managed to move it in and out on my own before." She bent down as if to push the thing along the dirt floor.

"I would like to help," he replied quietly and put his hand on the lip to still the tub. "You've done enough on your own." He glanced around them to emphasize his point. "Don't you think it's time you allowed someone to help?"

"You're ill."

"I can still lift a tin tub," he assured her and picked it up. "If you would be so kind as to get the doors." She conceded then because he had robbed her of the space between them and she had taken notice. She scurried around him and out into the sunlight.

Trevor was glad for the cold tub in his arms. It kept his hands busy and his mind grounded. "Evan." He said his brother's name almost like a curse. He shook his head at the thought of what his brother might have done. Then he walked out of the lean-to and carried the tub into the house.

Chapter Six

Maddie filled the tub with warm water, placed a couple of towels and a wash cloth on a chair nearby and a sliver of soap in the holder. Then she hung a fresh sheet up along the rafters, blocking the tub from view.

"There you go," she said and stepped off the chair, eyeing her handiwork.

"I didn't mean for you to go to so much trouble," Trevor said as he leaned against the bedroom doorjamb.

"It was no trouble really. I was out doing the wash."

He ran his hand along his handsome stubbled jaw. "I would go into town for a bath and a shave . . ."

"No, of course not," she said with indignation. He made her sound like an ogre. "You're far too weak. Now, get going before the water grows cold."

"Yes, ma'am," he said and saluted her. "Whatever you say, ma'am." She would have been mortified if it weren't for the attractive twinkle in his eyes.

"Don't you forget it," she called after him. Then she hurried out of the house. She had spent the last ten days caring for the man. They had been thrown into an unnatural intimacy. She had fixed his bath without a second thought.

She had to catch herself from offering to give him a

shave. That would have crossed a line she wasn't ready to cross.

She pulled the boiled laundry off the fire and readied it for the wringer, and tried not to think about the fact that he was naked in her tub. It had been so easy to touch him when he was ill. She had comforted him with cool cloths on his forehead, and given him short sponge baths to bring down his fever. If she was to be honest, she had already begun to miss the human contact.

It brought a purpose and meaning to her life and killed the loneliness that lingered.

She put a shirt into the wringer and began the arduous cranking process. Water streamed from the material. She thought about how things had not turned out the way she had planned. When she was living with her father, she thought she wanted nothing more than peace and quiet. She thought that there would be so much joy and comfort in being alone. No one to pick up after. No one to order her about. The only person in the whole world she had to answer to would be herself. That had been her idea of heaven.

In fact, she could not understand why her sister Beth craved male attention so much. Why would anyone leap from their father's house into that of another man's? So, she had been bold and vowed to live her life her way. Alone.

The lie had been both a blessing and a curse. While it allowed her to chart her own way in the world, it let her see that perhaps there was more to life than always doing things her way.

Now, with Trevor in her home, she found she actually liked the intimacy that formed between them. She was comforted by the sounds of another human being. The fact that the man was easy on the eyes didn't help matters.

She pulled the shirt before it fell out of the wringer and put it in the basket to be hung up. Then she put another article of clothing into the wringer. Always before, laundry went quickly. She only had two weekday outfits and a Sunday dress. Doing only her laundry was so much simpler than doing the laundry in her father's household. In fact she had patted herself on the back for being ingenious. Without husband there would be no children. Without children, laundry took one quarter of the time. There was more time for the things she loved to do.

But that got old fast. Now she took in laundry as a side business just to keep herself busy. When she baked, she sold her pies and cakes to the innkeeper in town. It wasn't any fun to cook unless there was someone else to enjoy her skills.

She looked up into the clear blue sky of fall and shook her head at her own silliness. Here she had thought to reinvent the world, and all she discovered was that the world was the way it was for a reason.

People need other people to stave off loneliness, to fight with, to confide in, and to share everything, good and bad.

She finished wringing the basket of clothes and picked it up, taking it to the line. Her fingers were red and chaffed from the wind and the water. She would have to put her special hand cream on tonight and wear gloves to bed. It didn't matter. She loved working. That was something else she had learned about herself. She wasn't the kind to lie around and eat candies all day.

She hung up the wet clothes and took down the dry. Tomorrow they would have to all be ironed. But for now, they were stiff and clean and smelled of sunshine.

She picked up the basket of dry clothes and walked toward the house. Trevor came through the door, pushing the rocker and dragging another chair behind him. She set her basket on the porch and went to help him. "What are you doing?" she chided. "You're not supposed to over-exert yourself."

"I'm not that weak," he countered. "I thought it would

be good to sit on the porch awhile and take in some fresh air."

She held the door for him and he set the chairs out. She crossed her arms over her chest. "For this you need two chairs?"

"One is for you," he said and patted the seat.

Maddie blinked. She didn't know what to say. No one had offered her a seat in the middle of the day. Ever. Her entire life people took her for granted. Even her brothers and sisters expected her to do the work while they loafed. The men who had courted her expected the same. It was one of the reasons she never wanted to marry.

"Oh," she said.

"Well?"

She looked at him blankly. "Well what?"

"Are you going to sit?"

She let go of the door. The screen banged as it snapped shut. "But it's the middle of the afternoon."

"Do you have someplace you need to be?"

"No."

"Then come sit with me a moment." He eyed her pointedly. "I can't sit until you do."

He looked worn out from pulling the chairs and she took pity on him. She sat in the closest chair, leaving him the rocker. He eased into the chair and slowly began to rock. "It is a lovely day, isn't it?"

"Yes," she said and clasped her hands on her lap. She took a deep breath and waited.

The sounds of day swirled around them. Chickens clucked nearby. The horses munched hay in the corral, flicking the flies off their backs with their tales. Birds flew overhead, some very high on their journey south. Some stayed low to the ground, eating seed and taking shelter where they could find it.

Maddie felt awkward sitting next to Trevor. She wasn't used to stopping in the middle of the day. She definitely wasn't used to conversation. Worse, the truth had been dragging on her shoulders. Yet, if she told him the truth now she would have to leave, and he was still too weak to be on his own.

She searched her brain for something to say. "How are you feeling?"

He rested his head back against the rocker and closed his eyes. "Much better thank you. So, what do you think?"

"About what?"

He ran his hand along his smooth chin. "About how I look?"

"You look nice," she blurted out, embarrassed. She wasn't used to talking to handsome men, let alone telling them they look nice.

He grinned knowingly at her and closed his eyes. "Tell me about you."

Something close to panic inched down her back. "What do you want to know?"

"Everything," he said and waved his hand. "We're practically family. Tell me everything."

"Hmm." Maddie looked out over the yard. The laundry snapped and flapped in the gentle breeze. Stall. She had to stall. "What in particular?"

"I know you have two sisters and two brothers."

"Three," she said quickly. "I have three brothers. There were six of us."

"What about your mother and your father?"

"Mama died just after Beth was born," Maddie said. "I'm the oldest girl so things kind of landed in my lap."

"I'm sorry."

"It was a long time ago," she said. "I'm used to the work and I don't remember the pain."

"That's how I feel about my father," Trevor said. "He died when I was thirteen. The pain isn't nearly as raw as when I think of my mother."

"But time will take care of that too," she said and put

her hand on his arm. She couldn't help it. She wanted to comfort him. The pain in his voice went straight to her heart. He glanced at her hand and she drew it away. The heat of embarrassment touched her cheeks. "I'm sorry."

"Don't be," he said gently. "We're family."

"Not yet," she said to hide the guilt that she felt. Her conscious nagged at her that this was the perfect time to tell him the truth. But she glanced at how pale he was. How tired he was from simply taking a bath and pulling out two chairs. She couldn't leave him yet.

"Don't be silly, you just spent nearly two weeks caring for me. The only way we could get closer is if we were courting."

"That's out of the question," she said. The thought was more appealing than she wanted to admit. But once the truth came out, the last thing Trevor would want to do was court her.

"Yes. It's out of the question."

The finality of his words stung. Did he suspect the truth? "Trevor—"

"I know. You are engaged to my brother."

"Right." Maddie had to shake herself mentally. "So, tell me, why did you decide to come home after all these years?"

"It was time," he said simply and rocked gently. "I guess I finally figured out that no matter where I ran to, I was always there."

"Why would you try to run away from yourself? You aren't a bad man."

"You don't know me," he said wearily.

"I know you well enough. You came home for your mother's funeral."

"Someone needed to see that she was properly buried."

"And that someone was you."

He rocked in silence. "During the war I did some things I'm not proud of, but I'm tired of running." He laid his head back and closed his eyes. "I woke up one morning and realized that I was a man without a home, without a dream."

"So you thought you'd come back and see what was left?"

"Everything looks as if she were still here," he said. "It's as if my Ma will come out that door at any moment and swat me upside the head for sitting here doing nothing."

"You loved her very much."

"Yeah. I put her through hell, but I loved her. That's why I came back. I wanted to ask her to forgive me for being such a fool."

"I'm sure she has," Maddie said. He looked so forlorn that it was so hard not to touch him.

He blew out a deep breath. "Once a long time ago, I dreamed of what I would do when I grew up. See that tree line over there?" He pointed to the edge of the north pasture.

"Yes."

"The farm runs nearly a hundred acres north. I was going to clear it two acres at a time. I figured by the time I was thirty, I'd have nearly thirty acres of good soil for planting."

"What would you have planted?"

"Corn, wheat, oats." He shrugged. "I think I would have grown all three and rotated them every year or so; first corn, then wheat, then rye." He glanced at her. "Pa told me that rye was good to grow and then till under the year before you let a field go fallow. Then, if you're patient, the field will produce twice as much oats as normal. I had it all figured out."

He pointed right. "Over there near that stream is a set of rocks. I thought it would be good to make a springhouse there with them. Something to keep the butter cool and the milk sweet. Next to that I'd make a new smokehouse. This one would be twice as big as my father's."

"Sounds ambitious."

He smiled. "Yeah, when I was young I knew everything. I had it all planned out."

"What happened?"

"My father died and I was mad at him." Trevor shrugged. "I was so mad I thought to heck with the farm. It can rot, just like he did."

"That's harsh."

"Grief is funny. You never know how you're going to react. Anyway, then the war broke out and I figured it was my ticket out of Boltonville."

"So you left and waited eight years to come back."

"Yeah." He closed his eyes. "It took me eight years to understand that those dreams were still alive inside me. The ironic part is, now I'm too beat up to fulfill them. Until I get over this illness, I could barely till the fields that are already cleared. Life takes its toll whether you want it to or not."

He opened his eyes and his silver gaze cut through her. "What about you, Madeline Morgan? What keeps you here, working your hands raw?"

She glanced down at her hands. From another's point of view they would look raw. She wished she had needlepoint or something to hide them with. "I like to stay busy."

"Really? Why aren't you married with five children of your own?" He studied her closely. "Oh, of course, you're waiting for my brother to return as promised. Loyal to the end I see."

"You make it sound as if that's bad." She sighed. "Contrary to what you might think, I'm neither a villain nor a saint. The truth is that no one ever came along who made me want to marry. Do you understand?"

"You mean since Evan."

"Of course."

"So, you're holding out for the best?"

"Yes," she said and smiled. "I'm looking for the best.

I've seen so many women desperate to marry that they give their lives to the first smooth-talking man who asks them. I vowed I would never do that."

He studied her a moment, his gaze far too clear. "Isn't that what you did?"

She stood up. His comments were too personal, too close to the truth. "What I've done and what I will continue to do is to live my life as I see fit. I want to live up to no one's expectations but my own."

"What expectations are those, Maddie? Do you know?"

"I have to finish the laundry and start supper," she said, dismissing his question. She was finished with the conversation.

"Maddie."

"What?"

He watched her, his silver gaze peering into her soul. "Thanks for sitting with me."

"I hope you like chicken and dumplings," she said, trying to put some emotional distance between them. "That's what we're having for dinner."

Later that night, Trevor sat near the fire. It was hard for him to sit so much, but while he knew he needed to get up and around, he also knew his own limitations. If he pushed himself too hard, he'd end up back in the bed. That was the last thing he wanted.

What he really wanted was to get to the bottom of this whole mystery. What was Maddie doing in his family home? Why did she stick to the story that she was engaged to his brother? It was clear to him that that story didn't jive. He wasn't well enough to really pursue it.

The silence in the house was thick and nearly uncomfortable. He pushed her this afternoon, and she had retaliated by claming up tighter than a swollen door on a rainy day.

He hated it. His own emotions warred inside him. He

needed to know the truth, but the idea that she was a squatter scared him. He liked her. It had been fun when their conversation was light. He liked her sense of humor. The way emotions played along her face. He liked her generous heart and her willingness to help everyone. No wonder the town had rallied behind her.

The last thing he wanted was to expose her as a liar, and yet he couldn't get out of his mind that fact that nothing about her fit.

He stewed on the problem in front of the fire. The cold silence between them grew awkward. If only he could get to know her better. Maybe if she learned to trust him, she would tell him the truth.

An idea struck him and he got up.

"Where are you going?" she asked, her curiosity showing.

"Not far." She accepted it and returned to her needlework. He went into his old bedroom and opened the trunk. There underneath the stacks of sheets and towels and preserved baby clothes was his father's fiddle.

Trevor pulled it out and ran his hand lovingly along the polished wooden back. He tweaked the strings and found them still tight. Then he dug back in the trunk until he found the bow.

It had been a long time since he'd played. He wasn't sure if he remembered how. He put the fiddle under his chin, placed his fingers into a key of C and ran the bow along the strings. The sound came out smoother than he imagined. Before he knew it, he had run through the scales, up and back down.

"You play," Madeline said.

He opened his eyes to find her standing in the doorway. "It's been years, but yes. Ma used to love music so Pa bought this fiddle and we all learned." He plucked at the strings. "I'm surprised it's in such good shape."

"I had it re-strung," she said. "I thought, if nothing else, one of my brothers could learn how to play."

He ran the bow across the strings and the fiddle cried a lonely tune. Then he let his fingers fly and the fiddle danced beneath him.

"Why don't you come out in the parlor and play."

"I'm pretty rusty."

"I don't mind. I like music too."

He followed her back into the parlor. She sat in a winged-backed chair and bent her head over her work. The firelight brought out the red in her hair, warming her complexion. She looked like a sculpture and he wanted to run his fingers along her face. He wanted to trace the outline of her cheekbones, the curve of her jaw, the sensual fullness of her lips.

He shook himself. He could never touch her. If she told the truth, then she belonged to Evan and one day Evan would return. If she lied, then he would expose her and she would not be able to tolerate him. He was stuck between a rock and a hard place.

Trevor poured his emotions into the fiddle. It wailed mournfully, crying for love lost. When he finished, he noticed that she wiped a tear off her cheek.

His heart softened. So, he played a slow sweet waltz. The music poured out of his soul and into his fingertips. It was as if he opened a dam, and emotions he hadn't realized he had spilled out. Like a man with a sore tooth, he explored the music locked inside him and time flew.

Somewhere along the way, she put down her needlework and sat mesmerized, tears running down her cheeks. He finished another song and she clapped. "Why aren't you playing concerts?"

"I'm not that good."

"I beg to differ." She wiped the tears off her cheeks. "You have me crying like a baby."

"I can fix that," he said, and played a sprightly dance

tune. She laughed and clapped and tapped her toes. It did his heart good to see her having so much fun. Her laughter healed some of the melancholy that had filled his soul.

He paused long enough to reach down and pull her from her chair. "Dance."

She pinkened with embarrassment. "By myself?"

"Sure," he said. "I won't watch. I'll play." He closed his eyes to prove his point. He played a country dance, one of the first dances everyone learns as children. He heard her tap her feet. Then slowly she began to trust that he wouldn't mock her. Her feet began to shuffle. By the end of the song, he could hear her moving about the room. His mind's eye pictured the movements that belonged to the song.

He pulled the last note from the fiddle and she clapped. Her expression was one of pure joy and sweetness, and his heart healed further, forgetting the mystery that kept them apart. "Do you know this one?" He started into a second dance.

"Yes!" she said, her tone excited. She sang the words as she lifted her skirts and tapped her feet. He bowed between measures and together they danced. First together, then apart. He turned left, she turned right. The song's tempo sped up. He challenged her by dancing faster. The glint in her gaze told him she was up to the challenge.

He stepped forward and back, she matched his rhythm. He turned right, she turned left. They promenaded across the parlor. Forward, and back, feet flying, fingers flying, he couldn't touch her and keep the music going. He couldn't touch her, but she understood without a word. Playing her part as if he had his hand on her waist, as if he twirled her, she danced.

Her skirts brushed his socked feet. The scent of rosewater rose and fell as she inched toward him then away. She smiled at him, her gaze flirty. The spirit of the dance was one of joy and sensual teasing.

He was trapped by the need to keep the dance going as

his fingers flew through the music, and his need to touch her, to keep growing her laughter and joy. If he stopped the spell would be broken.

But the longer the dance continued, the more he needed to catch her, to draw her into his arms and taste the promise in her eyes, the promise of joy and laughter and sweet comfort.

She stepped closer, then away. It became harder and harder to keep playing. The air in the room had grown thick with heat and scent and need and desire. Breathless, he stepped toward her and ended the song.

She stood so close her skirts wrapped around his legs. She smiled. Her bosom heaved as she tried to catch her breath. His heart raced, her scent surrounded him drawing him in. He tucked the fiddle under his arm, freeing one hand.

Reaching out, he cupped her cheek. She was warm and wonderfully alive. Her skin was like silk. Her gaze went from laughter to want and she leaned into his touch. The motion went straight to his heart.

Her lips parted and he leaned down, drawn to the feel of them on his thumb. Her eyes closed, her face tilted. She would not deny the kiss he so desperately needed. Just one taste he thought—one taste of the laughter in her soul.

The bow fell from his hands and rattled to the floor. She jumped at the sound and the moment was lost. He stepped back, putting a safe distance between them.

"What?!"

"I dropped the bow," he said and bent to retrieve it.

"Oh," she said, and stepped around the winged-back chair that held her needlepoint. "Well."

"Yes, well."

"Thank you. That was wonderful." Her fingers clutched the back of the chair.

"You're a good dancer. You should dance more often. It brings a lovely color to your cheeks."

She touched her abdomen and waved at her face. "I think I need more practice. It's left me breathless."

He struggled with his own breath, but not because of the dancing.

She glanced at him, suddenly realizing that he too struggled for breath. "Oh, no, you shouldn't have been dancing. You're still recovering."

"I told you exertion helps me get well faster."

"You look pretty pale. Sit, I'll get you some water." She turned to the kitchen. "Or would you prefer lemonade?"

He sat back down on the settee and watched her walk away. Clearly she had no idea how close he had come to kissing her. He frowned. If she had been in love with Evan, she should know the signs. It was as if she had never been close to a man her entire life. That thought bothered him. It deepened the mystery.

"Here," she said, and handed him a tall glass of lemonade. "Drink this."

He took the glass, letting his fingers touch hers. She jerked as if touched by heat. He glanced up to see her eyes widen momentarily and then she dropped her gaze to the floor. He smiled inwardly. No, she knew how close he had come to kissing her. She just hid it well.

He sipped the cool drink. "Thank you, but you really don't have to wait on me."

She picked up her needlework and clutched it to her. "Thank you for the music and the dance. I don't know when I've had such a good time." She took two steps back toward the kitchen. "My, my look at the time. Well, I'm off to bed now. Good night."

"Good night," he replied and watched as she fled to her bedroom. He took a long gulp of the lemonade. It was cool but not cool enough to quench the odd fires that burned inside him.

He shook his head. He had never been envious of his charming little brother. Until now.

Chapter Seven

Maddie closed her door behind her and leaned against it. The music from his fiddle still played in her mind. Her heart raced as she thought of dancing with Trevor. It had been fun. More than fun, it had been indescribable. She felt like Cinderella at the ball, dancing with the prince.

Awkward at first, then the music drew her in. When Trevor began to dance the male part, she entered into the spirit of the thing and played the female.

The dance was quick and flirty. His silver gaze flashed, his fingers flew, and his feet moved with a powerful grace. He was at once dangerous and safe for she knew that he couldn't touch her. Not if he was to continue with the music, and so she played.

She lifted her skirts to her ankles, swirled with the music, brushing ever so close to him and then away. He smelled like her soap, starch from when she ironed his shirt, and warm male. In essence he smelled like hers.

When she whirled, she would step so close she could feel his breath on the back of her neck. It did strange and wonderful things to her skin. The fiddle picked up the pace and so did she until she was breathless. Her skin sensitized to the heat that surrounded him. Her head became light with the intoxication of movement and the courtship of the dance.

When the music stopped, she stopped in place trying to catch her breath. He stood so close she could have rested her head on his shoulder. When he reached out and cupped her cheek, she could feel the pulse racing in his hand, the power and the latent strength of him.

Something inside her broke; she wanted, no, needed more and so she had leaned into his palm. It was so close, she could have tasted him and yet it wasn't close enough. His breath mingled with her breath, his dangerous gaze read into her lonely soul, calling her out of her shell.

She did the unthinkable. She closed her eyes and leaned forward, thirsting for his kiss.

A blush rushed over her now, heating her cheeks at the thought. She pressed her hands to her face, dropping her needlepoint on the floor. What if he had kissed her? Her knees buckled at the thought. She sat down on the cool wood floor and held her head. If he had kissed her, she would have kissed him back. As romantic and delicious as it sounded, she knew it would have thrown her out of the frying pan and into the fire.

She was supposed to be in love with his brother. What would he have thought of her if she had kissed him back? Even worse, what would the townspeople think when they found out she was cheating on her long lost love?

She dropped her forehead to the floor and let the coolness seep into her overheated blood. She was so darn attracted to Trevor. It was crazy, insane. What was she thinking?

All these years she had never met a man she was even remotely interested in. In fact, Beth's words echoed in her head—she had thought that perhaps there was something wrong with her.

Now she knew better. There was a man who could make her heart race, her hands tremble and her knees weak. Oh my, he was the wrong man. The only man she couldn't have.

Whatever was she thinking? She had to stop this madness. She had to stop it soon. As sweet and wonderful as the past few days have been, she couldn't help worrying that Beth was right. That whatever had brought Trevor home was also pushing Evan. The last thing she needed right now was for Evan Montgomery to come home.

She banged her head against the floor. She really was going to have to strangle Robert. This whole thing was all his fault.

She would have to tell everyone the truth and she would have to do it soon. The longer she waited the worse things would get. Now she would have to look Trevor in the eye, thank him for the dance, and then say, "Oh, by the way, I never dated Evan. It was all a big lie."

She could imagine the look on his devilishly handsome face. He'd be furious. The warmth and spark that she had seen tonight, the very thing that called to her soul would be gone, lost forever under the weight of her deceit.

Maddie pushed herself off the floor and threw herself on her bed. She had it bad. Here she was flinging herself on the bed just like Beth. Only Maddie was twenty-five years old, much too old to be experiencing her first crush, and much too smart to be caught up in such a terrible lie.

The fiddle started back up, a lovely sound in the middle of a dark lonely night. The music seeped from the living room through the kitchen and under her door. He played a slow seductive ballad. Maddie got up, drawn to her door. She stood there and listened, closing her eyes to savor the beauty of the music.

The fiddle called her out, but Maddie resisted its siren call. She knew that if she opened her door she would lose more than her innocence, she would lose her heart.

* * *

A stranger walked into the saloon in the middle of the afternoon. He looked lean and mean, like a wild thing that had been through too much. Anger seeped from his leathered skin. He was trail weary and wore a pair of six shooters that looked as if they were well used.

Rudy Harrison blinked through rummy eyes. He'd heard rumor of men like this. Men toughened by the war. Men who would as soon shoot you as look at you. Men like that never came to Boltonville, Wisconsin. There was nothing here for them. A small farming community, it barely kept the bank open.

The stranger ordered a beer, took the beverage and moved to the local poker game. Curious, Rudy took his drink and eased over where he could hear the conversation and yet remain a piece of the woodwork.

"You want in on the action?" Boss Pickens asked.

"Maybe," the stranger said. "If'n I do, I won't be usin' those cards." He pointed at the cards in Boss' hands.

"Why not?" Boss asked affronted. "They ain't marked."

"Ain't saying they are," the stranger said. "I'm just sayin' I ain't going to play using them."

Boss leaned back in his chair. "Well, sir, I don't believe I want to use any cards you have either."

The stranger shrugged an evil glint in his eye. "No skin off my back."

"I have a fresh pack," Henry Morgan said. The kid was only seventeen and already wise to the ways of the game. The stack of coins in front of him was proof he knew how to play the game. He pulled out a pack of cards, pulled the wrapper off them and slapped them on the table. "Ante up gentlemen. It's five card stud."

The stranger seemed to accept the new deck and Rudy felt the tension flow out of his body. He still didn't trust the man, but it didn't appear there'd be a gunfight today.

Four hands later, Boss asked, "What brings you to Boltonville?"

The stranger pushed back his dirty hat and called for another beer. "Looking for a buddy of mine."

"Who?"

"Evan Montgomery."

Henry Morgan straightened at the sound of Evan's name. "He's been gone since the war started."

"Really?" the stranger said, and played with his cards. His steely eyes narrowed further. "I heard tell he was headed back this way."

"Haven't seen him," Boss said, and threw more coins in the pot.

"Funny, I could have sworn he'd be in town by now."

"Henry here would know better than anybody if Evan was back or not. His sister's engaged to the man. Heard tell they're practically married."

The stranger's sharp gaze fell on the young man with the dark hair and midnight-blue eyes. "That right?"

Henry shrugged and concentrated on his cards. "Maddie doesn't talk about it," he said. "Read 'em and weep, gentlemen. A full house."

Boss threw his cards in with disgust. The stranger tossed his cards in as well and stood. "Thanks for the game."

"You going out to the Montgomery place?" Boss asked.

"Maybe," the stranger said as danger and anger oozed from his leather coat. Rudy wondered why the boy didn't see it. If it had been his sister, he'd have told the stranger to bug off.

"Not worth going out there now," Henry said with nonchalant calm. "It's Wednesday. Maddie comes into town on Wednesdays and tutors the Schyler boys."

"An' you're sure Evan ain't come back into town?"

"Sure as you're sitting there," Henry said and gathered up his winnings. "Besides, I doubt Evan will ever come back to town."

"Why's that?"

"He's been gone too long," Henry said and stood. He

looked the stranger in the eye. "He didn't even come back for his mother's funeral. Man like that ain't got call to return."

"Not even for your sister?"

"You leave my sister out of it," Henry warned.

The stranger grinned a wolfish grin. "What if I don't?"

Henry put his hand on his gun, but the stranger was faster. His pistol was out and aimed at Henry's heart.

"Whoa, there," Boss said, and put himself between the stranger's pistol and Henry. "Put the guns away."

"What gives you the right to tell me what to do?" the stranger asked.

Boss flipped open his coat to reveal the sheriff's badge he had pinned to his shirt. "Now, put the gun back."

The stranger put his guns away slow. Rudy wiped the cold sweat off his forehead. Henry Morgan was just a kid, but his pa, Robert Morgan, was known for protecting his own. Anything happens to a Morgan and there's hell to pay. Yep, people in this area treated the Morgans with respect. Of course, Robert held his brood to a higher standard. Sometimes it was whispered that he was too strict. That's why no one in town minded when lovely Madeline moved into the rundown Montgomery place.

They liked the idea of undying love, but more important, the town liked the fact that Maddie took such good care of the place.

"It's probably a good idea for you to go home, Henry," Boss said and sat back down at the table. He seemed relaxed, but Rudy saw that he kept his coat hitched up away from his gunbelt.

"Yes, sir," Henry said. He poured his winnings into a small leather pouch and headed out the door.

The stranger watched him go. His evil snake eyes took in far more than they should.

"Why don't you stay for another hand?" Boss said. It was an order not a suggestion.

The comment drew the stranger's attention. "You want to make sure I don't follow the kid."

"Let's just say it's better if we play another hand or two. It'll ease the tension in the room."

Rudy watched the stranger think on that a long minute before he finally threw a silver dollar into the pot. "Seven card draw."

"Now there's a game," Boss said and grinned. He pulled a long cigar out of his breast pocket, sniffed it, bit off the end, and put the rolled tobacco in his mouth. He nodded toward the cards and drew a match across the heel of his boot. "You deal."

The stranger picked up the cards and shuffled. Boss lit his cigar and puffed until aromatic smoke rings rose up over his head.

Rudy swallowed the last of his beer and figured the show was over. Besides, he needed another beer. He gave the stranger another once over. It might not hurt to be able to describe the guy. Robert Morgan might be happy for the information.

Maddie pulled a blouse out of the basket and placed it on the ironing board. She sprinkled the cloth with water and picked up one of the two hot irons she had resting over her fire. Maddie liked to iron outside whenever the weather permitted.

There was something nice about the cool air and bright sunshine of fall. Winter came early in Wisconsin and stayed late. There would be many times when she'd even have to hang the laundry inside. So she worked outside whenever she had the chance.

She pressed the collar and cuffs first. Then moved on to the left front panel of the shirt when Henry came riding into the yard. He pulled the horse up short and hopped off in one motion. "Maddie."

"Henry, what brings you this way?" She attacked the

material with the hot iron, careful not to keep it on too long and scorch the blouse.

"I've got news." He was out of breath, his face flushed.

Apprehension raced down Maddie's spine. She had waited too long to tell the truth. Evan was home.

She clamped her mouth shut to keep from jumping to conclusions. Instead of speaking, she covered her emotion by putting the iron back on the rack that stood above the fire and turning the tables on her brother. "Does Pa know you've been racing Applegate?"

"How'd you—" Henry glanced at his horse. The animal had flecks of foam on his sides. "Never mind. I've got news. News bigger than my pushing Applegate although that horse can run, Maddie."

"I know what he can do, I've taken him out a time or two myself," Maddie replied and crossed her arms over her chest. "But you know that Pa restricted you from driving him so hard."

"Shoot, it was for a good reason."

"Let's hope so," Maddie said, schooling herself for his big news. Henry was a bit dramatic. It allowed him to play a good game of poker, and tell a good story. Maddie prayed his news was just that—a good story.

She picked up the blouse and placed the right panel on the board. Then she sprinkled water on it and grabbed the hotter of the two irons. "Now, what is the news?"

Henry let go of Applegate's reins and let the horse roam the yard. He moved in close to Maddie and shoved his hands in his pockets. "That shirt his?"

She glanced from her brother to the man's undershirt on top of the basket of clothes. "Yes," she said and tried to hide the blush that threatened to rush up her cheeks.

Henry glanced toward the house. "Is he still sick?"

"He's recovering, but he's still pretty weak," she replied. "Tell Pa he can send Beth over if he's worried about it."

"If he's worried, he won't be for long," Henry said. "There's a stranger in town."

"Really?" She ignored the panic that edged through her at his words. Instead she attacked the blouse with the iron.

"Yeah, I didn't like the looks of him right off. He was kind of shifty eyed and suspicious."

Maddie straightened. "You need to quit reading those dime novels."

"No, I mean it. He looked just plain mean and you know what?"

"What?"

"He said he was looking for Evan Montgomery."

Maddie felt that news in the pit of her stomach. It was almost as bad as what she feared. She grabbed the ironing board and saved herself from dropping the iron and burning a hole in her best blouse. "What?" She barely got the word out. Dread nearly drove her to the ground.

"Yeah, he comes into the saloon and asks if we'd seen Evan Montgomery. Boss and I tell him, no. Evan hasn't been back since he left for the war. Right?"

"Right," Maddie managed to squeak out. Her mind raced over the implications. Beth's intuition had been right. Evan was on his way here. Oh my, she needed to fix this and she needed to fix it soon.

"Well, he says he heard rumor that Evan was coming back home. He says he needs to talk to him."

"So, Evan is coming home?"

"That's what this guy says. From the look of him, I think he was serious."

Maddie tried to breathe. What she needed to do right now was breathe. Then she could think. Then she could figure out what it was she was going to have to do to keep her father from killing her. Where was her brother Robert when she needed him? Her mind darted about desperate.

"Did you tell, Pa?"

"Nope," Henry said and shook his handsome head. "I

rushed right over here. I figured you've waited so long for Evan. You should be the first one to know he was coming home. I figured you might want to freshen up or something."

"Something?" Maddie realized she was still holding the iron and put it down.

"Yeah, you know, put on a pretty dress or something. I mean, you don't want his first sight of you looking like a washerwoman, do you?"

What she wanted to do was smack her brother, but she couldn't. He was right. She'd been doing laundry all day and so she was dressed in an old skirt, a simple blouse and a large apron. Her hands were red and raw. Her hair had straggled out of its updo. Shoot, she did look like a washerwoman.

She glanced at the house. What did Trevor think of how she looked? As if he knew she was thinking about him, he stepped out on the porch and leaned against the post.

It was the first time she had seen him since last night. Embarrassed, Maddie had gotten up early and kept herself outside doing chores all day. Anything to avoid the conversation they were going to have. The one where she would have to talk about why she had almost kissed him the night before.

Standing there on the porch, Trevor looked more handsome than any man she'd ever seen in her whole life.

"What are you lookin' at?" Henry followed her gaze and straightened. "Oh. He doesn't look too weak to me."

"He has boots on," Maddie said. It was silly. Every man wore boots, but Trevor hadn't had his on since he'd gotten sick. It was clear he was trying very hard to appear normal.

"Hey, Maddie, do you want me to tell him about Evan coming home?"

"No!"

Henry looked at her as if she had lost her mind.

"I'll tell him," Maddie said, firmly. "Why don't you take

Applegate into the barn, give him a rubdown and a handful of oats?"

"Sure." Henry said with a shrug. "Hey, do you have anything good in the house?"

"I made an apple pie."

"Great. Let's celebrate." Henry grinned at her. "I'll be in for my piece as soon as Applegate's taken care of."

Maddie couldn't take her eyes off of Trevor. For the first time in days he looked like the dangerous man who had burst into her home. It made her heart flip and her hands tremble. She had to tell him.

Her mouth went dry as he started toward her. Maddie realized that she had been staring and the heat of embarrassment raced over her. She hid it by quickly piling the folded and ironed laundry into a clean basket.

She knew the moment he stepped within a few feet of her. For some reason, she was unusually aware of him. She caught herself taking a deep breath when the scent of bay rum and warm man drifted her way.

She had to stop acting like a lovesick schoolgirl. This man had every right to hate her. She lied to him and used his family and his family's home.

"Need some help?" he asked, and leaned against the laundry pole.

"No, thank you," she said curtly. She felt bad the minute the snippy words came out of her mouth. It wasn't his fault. She was the one with the house of cards about to come falling down around her.

He surveyed the yard. She worked as quickly as possible on the clothes, gathering up the unfinished things. The rest of the laundry would have to wait another day. She planned on going inside and changing her clothes. If Henry was right and she was about to meet her doom, then the last thing she wanted was to look like a washerwoman.

"Who's the kid?" Trevor asked.

"That's my brother, Henry. He's the youngest boy."

"How old is he?"

"Seventeen."

"He rides that horse like an expert."

"It's a Morgan trait," she said and folded the last bit of linen. "We're weaned on horses. Papa's considered the best horseman in the area."

She bent down to pick up the stacked baskets. He beat her to it. For a brief moment they were both bent over, face to face. He was close enough to kiss. His skin was clean and freshly shaven. He smelled so good it hurt.

"I got it," he said, his voice oddly deep.

"But you're—"

"No longer an invalid," he replied and hefted the baskets. Maddie knew it was pretty heavy. Not as heavy as when the clothes are wet, but heavy enough. She usually took the baskets inside one at a time, but she had been in a hurry.

"At least let me take one."

"I'm fine. Could you get the door?"

"Okay." She walked with him to the porch and opened the door.

He stepped inside and put the baskets down on the table, separating them. He rested on the last basket and Maddie hurried around and pulled a chair out from under the table. "Here, sit."

"I'm fine. If I can dance all night, I can bring in a few baskets of laundry."

"Sure you can," she said airily, not wanting to be reminded of the intimacy of last night. "Henry asked for a piece of pie. I highly doubt you want to eat your pie standing up." She pulled the baskets off the table and stowed them in the cupboard.

"You made a pie?"

"Apple, I made it this morning." She pulled the pie out of the pie safe, gathered three plates, a knife, and a spatula to scoop it out with. "I like cheddar with mine. How about you?"

"I like pie."

"I like pie too," Henry said as he burst into the house. "Maddie makes the best apple pie in three counties."

Trevor cocked a dark eyebrow at her. "She does?"

"Oh, yes," Henry said and pulled out a chair to sit down.

"Wash!" Maddie ordered as she cut the pie.

Henry got back up slow and embarrassed. "Right."

"I won a blue ribbon at the county fair last month," Maddie found herself bragging. She shook her head. What did she think? She could seduce him with pie and get him to forget that she was a liar?

She put two plates of pie down on the table.

"Aren't you going to have any?" Trevor asked.

"I'm not very hungry." It was suddenly very true. She was about to meet her doom and here she was dishing out apple pie. What was she thinking?

"Did Maddie tell you the news?" Henry said as he simultaneously swung his body into the chair and took a bite of pie.

"Tell me what?" Trevor asked.

"About the guy in town."

Trevor looked at Maddie. Maddie suddenly wished she had something to do with her hands. Her doom was at hand and she stood here lost, looking like a washerwoman.

"What guy?" he asked.

"Henry said he met a man in town who claims to know Evan."

Trevor turned his attention on Henry. "Did he tell you his name?"

"Nope," Henry said between bites of pie. "He said he was a friend of your brother's and was looking for him."

"What for?"

"Don't know. He said he heard Evan was coming home and so he wondered if he were back yet."

"What did you tell him?"

"Boss told him that Evan hadn't been back since before

your ma died," Henry said and finished off his pie. He pushed his plate back with a smile. "This guy didn't take that very well, but Boss calmed him down. Anyway, I thought maybe Maddie should know about him. He seemed to want to talk to her about Evan."

"Why would he want to talk to me?" Maddie asked. Her voice sounded breathy. She could barely make out a syllable. Maddie pulled out a chair to sit down before she fell down.

"Boss told him you were Evan's fiancée."

"Why did he do that?"

"Because everyone knows that you are," Henry said and looked at her as if she had lost her mind.

"Yes," Trevor said and turned his attention on her. "Everyone knows it. Isn't that right?"

Maddie stood up. "It's getting late, Henry. You need to get home before Pa sends Amelia after you. You know how upset she gets if she has to give up her books to come find you."

"Yeah," Henry said and stood. "Last time she nearly tweaked my ear off." He rubbed his right ear as if he could still feel the pain. "Gotta go. Nice to meet you, mister." Maddie was glad to see her brother remember enough of his manners to say that before he ran out the door. Henry shook Trevor's hand and left with a grin.

An odd silence crept through the kitchen, filling the space from the bottom up. Maddie busied herself putting the pie and things away. She felt Trevor's gaze on her the whole time.

"How are you today?" she asked when she couldn't take the silence any more.

"Good. I did some walking. It looks like you had corn growing in the south forty."

She turned toward him and brushed a loose hair away from her face. "I didn't grow anything. I leased the field out to Tom Blake. I have the money if you want it."

He waved his hand. "Keep it."

"But it's your land."

"Not according to the mayor."

"That was before you came home."

"And now?"

"Now it's your land," she said. "You can plant whatever you want on it." She took his empty plate, rinsed it and set it in the sink.

"You're in early," he commented. "Looks like you still have ironing to do."

"I do, but it'll have to wait. Right now I have to go into town. I tutor on Wednesdays."

"Oh." He studied her until she turned on him.

"What?"

"Are you going to want me to bring the hipbath inside?"

"Why? It's not Saturday."

"No, it's not, but if your little brother is to be believed, my brother is coming home."

"So?"

"So, I figured you might want to get gussied up or something."

"What is it with you guys?" Maddie muttered under her breath. "A gal can't run around dressed in her Sunday best every day. Nothing would get done."

He contemplated her a bit too long. "You do a lot around here, don't you?"

"I like to keep busy."

"I've never seen the larder so full."

"It was a good year."

"You had no idea either of us Montgomerys would be coming home and yet you acted as if we simply went off for a week to Chicago."

A blush rushed up her cheeks. "I like to be prepared."

"Really?" He got up. He stalked her through the kitchen like a predator certain of his prey. Maddie held very still, refusing to back away. He would not intimidate her. If only she could get her heart to realize that.

He reached out and brushed the hair away from her cheek. "Were you prepared for me?"

"No," she replied honestly. She could feel herself tremble at his touch. It was all she could do not to lean into him. Not to tell him the whole tale and beg him to love her anyway.

"You are beautiful even when you're working." His words were a whisper that caressed her skin. "Especially when you're working. You take such good care of everything around you, tell me, Madeline, who takes care of you?"

"No one."

"That needs to change. Everyone needs someone to take care of them." He tucked her hair behind her ear, his fingers sending gooseflesh down her side. "Let someone take care of you."

"Who?" she asked, desperate to hear him say that he should be the one. He let his gaze wander over her face. She bit her lip and waited for his response. It seemed as if time stood still.

Finally, he took a step back. "Evan, of course," he said and cleared his throat. "I'm glad to hear he's on his way home. Then I don't have to worry about you being alone, do I?"

The suspicion in his eye got her back up as disappointment washed over her. She lifted her chin and blinked back the hurt. "Evan or no Evan," she began, "you needn't worry yourself over me, Trevor Montgomery. I'm used to taking care of myself." Then she turned and escaped into her bedroom. She leaned against the closed door and shook her head.

Evan was coming home. She put her hand on her throat. The noose was getting tighter.

Chapter Eight

"**M**addie! Yoo-hoo, Maddie Morgan!"

Maddie glanced over her shoulder to see Mrs. Selis and Mrs. Lance bearing down upon her. She stopped short and looked around. There was nowhere to run, nowhere to hide. The most prudent thing was to simply let them overtake her.

"Maddie," Mrs. Selis said as she approached. "We all heard the news."

"What news?" Maddie knew it was best to let the ladies think they had the upper hand.

"Why, the good news, of course," Mrs. Lance said.

"Excuse me?"

"Oh, my, you haven't heard," Mrs. Selis surmised and took Maddie by the arm. "I have it from a very reliable source that Evan Montgomery is coming back to town."

"Evan?" Maddie clutched her tutor books to her chest. "Really? When?"

"Why, any moment now," Mrs. Selis said. "You must be thrilled."

"Whatever will you wear?" Mrs. Lance said and glanced down at Maddie's clothes.

Maddie had changed into a decent skirt, blouse and

close-fitted jacket. She wore a proper hat and gloves. She refused to let anyone tell her she still looked like a washerwoman now. "This is my second best outfit," Maddie said. "I'm sure I look fine."

"You look darling," Mrs. Selis said and tugged Maddie along. "Just pinch your cheeks, dear, it will put some color in them."

"Oh, and bite your lips a little," Mrs. Lance said. "It helps them to stand out."

Maddie shook her head. "I have a tutoring session I must attend. We can talk about this later."

"Oh, Maddie, whatever are you thinking?"

"Yes," Mrs. Lance said. "What are you thinking?"

"I'm thinking the boys are waiting for me."

"Nonsense," Mrs. Selis said. "I'm certain their mother has heard the news. The last thing she will expect is for you to show up at her door to teach her boys."

"Why?" Maddie was becoming confused.

"Because, she will expect you to run straight home and see that you look your best. After all, Evan could be at your father's house right now . . . looking for you."

"But—"

"No buts," Mrs. Selis said, and pulled Maddie through the streets toward her father's house. "We have something for you, dear."

"Yes, a wonderful something," Mrs. Lance said and clapped her lace-gloved hands. "Wait until we get to your father's house."

Maddie dragged her feet. "What is going on?"

"Well, it wouldn't be a surprise if we told you," Mrs. Selis said. She gave a little laugh that reminded Maddie of a chicken's cackle.

Maddie's heart pounded in her chest. "Have you seen Evan? Is he here?"

"Oh, it's even better than that," Mrs. Lance said.

"Even better?" Maddie didn't like the sound of that. The

ladies pulled her toward her father's house. They opened the gate of the whitewashed picket fence that surrounded the house and pushed Maddie through.

The door swung open and Beth came out grinning like a loon. "Good, you have her," Beth said. "Come on, Maddie, there is something you must see."

Maddie swallowed hard and lifted her skirts as she mounted the stairs. "A good something, I hope."

"Of course," Beth said with a giggle.

Maddie stepped through the door and into the sound of applause. She blinked and waited a second to let her eyes adjust to the dim interior of the house. The house was filled with women. It seemed everyone in town was there and they were all smiling the same knowing smile. Maddie knew a moment of sheer terror.

"Let me take your things." Mrs. Poole stood just inside the door and took Maddie's books and hat.

"What is going on?" Maddie asked her in a low whisper.

Mrs. Poole raised an eyebrow, but would not tell. Maddie turned to face the crowd that gathered in the parlor and currently spilled into the hallway. If she was not mistaken, the entire ladies brigade of Boltonville was standing in her father's home.

It wasn't a good sign.

"They started showing up the moment they heard," Amelia said as she rounded a corner with a tray of refreshments in her hands. "I had no idea news could travel so fast."

"Me, neither," Maddie agreed. She turned her attention to the ladies. "Hello, everyone."

The crowd stood and surged toward her. All of the ladies seemed to speak at once, congratulating her and wishing her well, and telling her how they heard the news from this person or that. The din that resulted made Maddie's ears ring.

She smiled and nodded and swiped a small glass of punch off the tray Mrs. Poole brought out. She took a fortifying swallow and found herself wishing there was something stronger inside.

"Ladies, ladies, please," Mrs. Selis said and clapped her hands to quiet everyone down. "Thank you." She turned toward Maddie and beamed. "Maddie, we are all here today to congratulate you on your forthcoming wedding."

Maddie swallowed her punch wrong. She couldn't breathe. She turned her head and tried to hide the coughing as much as possible. Mrs. Lance pounded her on the back while Mrs. Selis pulled Maddie's arms over her head.

"Arms up, dear," Mrs. Selis said. "That's a girl."

"My wedding?" she squeaked when she could finally speak.

"Of course, your wedding," Beth said. "Are you okay?"

"Sure," Maddie said after she caught her breath. She handed her cup to Beth. "I'm sorry, Mrs. Selis, but I have no idea what you are talking about." The ladies all smiled knowingly at her and horror eased down Maddie's spine. "What?"

"We all know that Evan is on his way home at this very minute," Mrs. Selis said. She clasped her hands in front of her as if Maddie was simply being silly.

"You have been so patient with him. So loyal and loving we just know he'll be over the top when he sees you," Mrs. Lance added.

"The way we see it is that you two kids have been apart long enough. The sooner you can be married the better," Mrs. Selis concluded.

"The sooner, the better?" Maddie could barely get the words out of her throat.

"Of course you don't want to appear too eager," Mrs. Lance said.

"No, I certainly don't want to appear too eager."

"He will have to woo you at least a little," Mrs. Selis said.

"Yes," Maddie agreed, grabbing a hold of the idea and

running with it. "He should feel like he has to woo me. It wouldn't be right for me to fall into his arms the first moment I see him." She glanced at the crowd. "Men appreciate you more if they have to work a little to get you. You know, the thrill of the hunt, etcetera."

"Pish, after eight years, we've decided he's been out hunting long enough," Mrs. Selis declared and the crowd murmured its agreement. "The boy will simply have to take you in his arms and declare his undying love."

There were several sighs and some encouraging whispers.

"We will give him two days to realize what a treasure you are," Mrs. Selis said. "Then we will have us a big beautiful wedding."

"Two days," Maddie protested. "That isn't enough time to have a proper wedding. Why, there's the cake, a dress, flowers . . ."

"That's where we come in dear," Mrs. Selis said, and grinned at her like a cat that just finished off the canary. "Since your sweet mother died, we ladies have felt like the least we can do is to step in and take her place. Especially with such details as a wedding. Ladies." Mrs. Selis waved her hand and the crowd parted.

There in the middle of the room stood Mrs. Armstrong the local seamstress. In her hands was a lovely confection of satin and lace. Mrs. Armstrong held up the gown. It had small puffed sleeves, and a squared off bodice that pointed into a wide hooped skirt. The material shimmered in the afternoon light. It wasn't white. It was a pale silver blue, the very color of Trevor's eyes.

Maddie couldn't help it. She was drawn to the beautiful gown. The crowd smiled as she stepped forward and fingered the fine material. Satin and lace meshed into the most exquisite gown she had ever seen. "Who?"

"We've been working on it for years," Mrs. Armstrong said. "See the embroidered pattern?"

Maddie took in the fine silver flowers that cascaded down the outer skirt. "It's lovely."

"The ladies started working on it the month that we convinced your father to let you wait. We didn't think it would be long and so we worked on it every time we got together."

"But then the months turned into years and so we got creative with the lace and all," Mrs. Lance said.

"It's lovely," Maddie said, tears welling up in her eyes. It was clear these ladies meant to show how much they cared for her. It made the lie all that more horrible.

"Try it on," Mrs. Selis said.

"I couldn't," Maddie protested. She ran her fingers over the hand-made lace at the edge of the sleeves. The tiny embroidered flowers on the satin. "It's too much."

"Try it on," Mrs. Armstrong said and handed the dress to Maddie. "I think you'll be excited to see how well it fits."

Maddie took the dress in her hands and held it up against her. It was a dress made for a princess. She didn't know what to say. She didn't know what to do. She glanced around and took in the waves of beaming faces. How could she tell them it was all a lie?

"Come on," Beth said and took her elbow. "Everyone has been dying to see you try it on."

"It's too much," Maddie said.

"You will try it on," Mrs. Selis ordered. "Amelia, Beth, take your sister into the dining room and help her with the gown."

Maddie let her sisters pull her out of the crowd. They closed the pocket door that separated the parlor from the dining room. The crowd outside the door burst into sound as the ladies' excitement grew.

Maddie clutched the gown in cold fingers. Beth beamed from ear to ear.

"Isn't it lovely?" she said and sighed. "I always dreamed

of such a dress and to think the ladies made it for you.
Why, they've been working on it for years. I can't believe
they were able to keep the secret."

"I can't believe you didn't suspect they were up to this,"
Amelia said as she unbuttoned Maddie's jacket.

"I thought the farm would satisfy them," Maddie said.
She was still stunned.

Beth grabbed the dress from Maddie and danced around
the dining room. "It is the prettiest thing I have ever seen
in my life."

"I don't deserve it," Maddie said as Amelia stripped her
of her jacket, blouse and skirt.

"You deserve it more than anyone else in the whole
town," Amelia said. "You've done nothing but care for
everyone. They wanted to pay you back in a good way.
They want to see you happy and in love and well . . .
happy. It's their way of mothering you, and you have to
let them. Now, Beth, bring me that dress."

Beth handed the dress to Amelia. Maddie allowed her
sister to pull the lovely material over her head. "No, you
don't understand. I really don't deserve this."

"A girl as unwaveringly loyal as you deserves this
dress," Amelia said. She moved around to the back and
began to do up the long line of pearl buttons in the back.

Maddie stroked the beautiful material. Just wrapping herself in it made her feel like a princess.

"You look like Cinderella," Beth said and clapped her
hands. "Oh, Maddie, isn't it all so romantic?"

Maddie thought about the hours of work that had gone
into the gown and her heart sank. How could she tell them
the truth now? She closed her eyes and tried to ignore the
crowd outside the room. "I can't take this."

"Nonsense," Beth said, suddenly sounding like their
mother. "You look lovely."

"Really, Maddie," Amelia said behind her. "You are a
vision."

"No, you don't understand."

"I understand that there are thirty ladies outside that door, who have been keeping this dress a secret for two years," Amelia said. "Now you're going to go out there and tell them how much you love it."

Maddie glanced over her shoulder at her younger sister. "Goodness, you sounded like Mama."

Amelia smiled knowingly. "You're not the only one who paid attention around here."

Beth was at the doors. "Ready or not," she said and flung the doors wide. Every pair of eyes in the room turned to look at Maddie.

She put on her best smile and walked bravely out into the parlor. The ladies surrounded her, cooing and ahhing and all speaking at once.

"Ladies, ladies," Mrs. Selis said, and clapped her hands to get their attention. "Please, let's hear what Madeline has to say. Maddie?"

"It's perfect," Maddie said. She held out her arms and twirled so everyone could see. Her heart pounded at the attention, and the sure and certain knowledge that this would be the only time she wore this lovely dress. The truth had to come out sooner or later.

"Let me see, let me see," came a snappy old voice from the back of the crowd. "Out of my way." The crowd parted to let Mrs. Addlestone through. The woman was nearly eighty years old. She could barely walk, and so sat in a wheelchair. Her nurse pushed through the crowd.

Maddie waited, frozen to the spot. Ever since she was a young girl, Mrs. Addlestone had been torturously honest. So honest in fact, the old lady could get to the truth in any story merely by looking at you. Maddie prayed she didn't have liar written all over her forehead.

She stood still while the old woman looked her up and down. Her glasses perched ceremoniously on the tip of her hooked nose. "Maddie."

"Yes, Mrs. Addlestone?"

"Maddie, you look like your dear departed mama in that dress," the old woman declared. "How do you feel?"

"Like a princess."

"Don't give me that horse-pucky," the old lady said and swatted Maddie with her fan. "How do you feel?"

Maddie tried not to look her directly in the eye. For some reason direct eye contact with Mrs. Addlestone could wring the truth out of the most hardened criminal. "Well, I must admit I'm amazed." Maddie swallowed.

"You're amazed?"

"Yes, I'm amazed that I had no idea the ladies had done this. It is a lovely gown and it fits perfectly."

"Nonsense," Mrs. Addlestone declared. "There's nothing to be amazed at. It was the next logical thing for these quilters." She leaned in closer at Maddie. "We want to know how you feel."

"How I feel about . . ."

"The news silly," Mrs. Addlestone said and snapped her fan shut with disgust. "How do you feel about the rumor that Evan Montgomery is coming home? How long had he been away?"

"Eight years."

"Eight years," Mrs. Addlestone said and shook her gray head. "He should have been dead by now."

Maddie had to stop herself from agreeing with the older woman. Really, Evan should have been dead. It would make everything so much easier.

Guilt washed through her at the thought. It wasn't Evan's fault she had made up this lie.

"Well?"

"Well, what?" Maddie parroted, trying to find her sisters in the crowd.

Mrs. Addlestone stomped her cane. Maddie swore she would have shaken her if she could have reached her. "How do you feel about the news?"

"Shocked, I guess," Maddie said. It was always best not to stray too far from the truth. "Nervous, really."

"Now there's the honest truth," Mrs. Addlestone said with triumph. "I knew you had it in you girl." She patted Maddie's hand. "Nothing wrong with being nervous. No telling what the boy looks like anymore. Could have gotten both arms and legs shot off in the war."

Maddie blinked at the image of a wounded man in a wheelchair.

"But here you are, still filled with your true love. Gonna marry him anyway, ain't 'cha?" She cackled. "A woman's got to do what a woman's got to do. Ain't that right?" she asked the general assembly.

Maddie was horrified to see the smiles and laughter brought on by that comment. It was all she could do not to turn tail and run. Why, she could lift these skirts up, dash out the back and be gone within minutes.

"Don't listen to that old biddy," Mrs. Selis said and took Maddie's arm. "I'm sure Evan is right as rain, isn't that right, Mrs. Lance?"

"Right as rain," Mrs. Lance parroted with a silly smile on her face. "You look so pretty, honey, it brings tears to my eyes." She lifted a handkerchief to the corner of her eye as if to prove her point.

"It's so romantic," Beth said with a sigh. "And to think, you don't have to worry about a thing. Absolutely everything has been taken care of."

"Absolutely everything?" Maddie muttered.

"Yes, Mrs. Selis and Mrs. Lance have the chapel booked for two days from the day Evan comes home, don't you?"

"Yes, we do," Mrs. Lance said.

"Mrs. Smith is making you a three-tiered cake. It has to be that big because everyone in town will be coming," Mrs. Selis said. "Your sisters are both prepared to act as brides-maids. The ladies brigade plans a pot luck, and Sam Snyder said he and his fellows will be happy to play the fiddle and such for entertainment."

Maddie's thought turned to Trevor and the beautiful music he made just for her in the cabin.

"Isn't it perfect?" Beth gushed. "Why, I am so jealous."

"Yes, everything is just perfect," Maddie muttered. *Perfectly awful.*

"Actually, I'm not envious at all, I'm happy. With you finally married, maybe Papa will see that I am no longer a baby. Why, he will have to take my beaus more serious when they come calling."

Maddie didn't know what to say. Somehow Beth managed to make this whole charade about her. Maddie didn't have time to sigh before Mrs. Selis took her by the elbow.

"Come on now, Maddie, be a good girl and mingle with your guests. I want to show off the dress."

"Yes, of course," Maddie muttered and allowed herself to be drawn into the crowd. It really was a lovely dress. Perhaps they'd bury her in it after they strung her up when the truth finally came out.

Chapter Nine

T revor sat on the porch and played his fiddle. He let the instrument sing out the melancholy he felt. Maddie had left early in the afternoon. It was near to dark and she had yet to return.

He waited on the porch, torn between wanting her to return and the vague hope that the threat of Evan's impending return would send her running back home. If she ran, then it would be as he suspected all along. Madeline didn't really love Evan. She had just used his brother as a way to worm her way out of having to get married.

He'd spent the afternoon wandering around the place. It was clear that the farm was too much for his current state of health. He thought of Evan's return. His brother was younger and probably healthier. If they could put their differences aside, they may be able to make a go at it.

There was just one problem. If Maddie wasn't lying, then she and Evan would eventually marry. That would leave him living with two newlyweds. One of which held his heart in the palm of her hands.

Trevor ground his teeth at the thought of Maddie and Evan. He couldn't stay here if they stayed, and he couldn't take the place away from Madeline, not after her years of hard work. She might be lying about her supposed place as Evan's fiancée but she had taken good care of the place.

Trevor frowned. He realized that he wanted her to be lying about being Evan's fiancée to justify the deep attraction he felt for her. But if she was lying, it would mean she wasn't who she seemed. Right now it seemed that she belonged here more than he did, heck more than Evan did.

Which could only mean one thing—she was Evan's fiancée.

That thought hurt him deeper than he wanted to know about. The thought that her gentle hands, her courageous heart and her sweet mouth all belonged to his brother.

The idea of Evan having it all made him want to put his fist through someone's head. As far as Trevor knew, Evan never gave a lick about the farm. It seemed he really didn't give a lick about Madeline either or he would have come home well before now.

Trevor balled his fist and put the fiddle down. Evan had been Ma's favorite, Evan with the winning smile and the gaggle of girls that always followed him about. Beautiful, spoiled Evan.

Heck, even Trevor used to indulge his baby brother. It was easy. Evan had been like a puppy chasing at his heels. But now, Trevor blew out a long breath and uncurled his fists. Now it seemed Evan had what Trevor wanted most, health, home and Madeline.

He closed his eyes. It was useless to fight it. The deed was done. Maddie didn't belong to him, but Maddie belonged to the farm. He wouldn't be the one responsible for taking that away from her. If only she would tell him the truth. If only that truth had nothing to do with her love for his brother. Why, then he'd figure something out. He was a smart man and used to getting what he wanted.

Yes, that's it. If she did come back, then he would push Madeline until the truth came out. He would help her figure out how to fix everything.

Trevor shifted as his bones began to ache. His resolve was firmly in place. He'd do whatever it took to get the truth out of her. He prayed the truth was that she didn't love Evan.

He stood up when he heard a horse approaching. Relief washed over him as Maddie rode out of the sunset, her glorious hair ablaze. She sat straight and true. Her mare cantered with delight and Maddie handled her like an expert.

A rush of lust and longing plowed through him. He needed to do something to keep from running to her and gathering her in his arms. He picked up his fiddle and stowed it away, all the time reminding himself that she hadn't told him the truth about anything and he needed the truth. He glanced up to see that she stopped the horse in front of the stables and hopped off. Her cheeks were flushed in the draining light. Her breathing rushed as if she had been racing.

Trevor found himself drawn to her. She was alone and she was here and Evan hadn't arrived yet. He made his way across the lawn.

"You were gone a long time," he said. It came out like an accusation and she looked over her shoulder at him.

"I got sidetracked." She pulled the reins and led the horse into the barn.

Trevor followed. "What does that mean?" He suddenly went from accusation to pure jealousy. He knew he had no right to these feelings, but they were there anyway. He opened the stall door for her.

"It means I was waylaid by the Boltonville Ladies Brigade," Maddie said. She pulled the bridle off the mare and poured a cup of oats into the feeding trough. Then she unhooked the saddle.

"The ladies brigade?" He couldn't help but sound incredulous.

"Yes, the ladies brigade. If you knew Mrs. Selis and Mrs.

Lance, the leaders, you would understand that there is no getting around them." She went to lift the saddle off.

Trevor stepped in, trapping her between him and the horse. His hands covered hers. He meant to help her with the saddle. But once he got close he froze. She smelled so good. Her body fit perfectly under his arms. If he just leaned forward a little, he would be able to feel her curves.

The idea was so tempting it drew every thought out of his head. He inched closer. How does one take a forbidden woman into their arms? You don't was the answer and he knew it. Still the pause was so long and drawn out. His body screamed just to touch her. It may be the last time he ever got to and yet . . .

"I'll get it," he managed to say through gritted teeth. She let go of the saddle, her capable hands sliding away from his. He had to touch her when he pulled the saddle off the horse. It was only a brief instant, but it heated the air in the stall until he could barely breathe.

Trevor covered it well. He took the saddle and crossed the barn, to throw it up on a nearby stall.

"Thanks," she said behind him.

He closed his eyes and worked to get a hold of his emotions. "It was nothing." He caught his breath and turned to face her.

She had the blanket off her horse and was brushing the mare. Trevor watched the way she worked. Careful, graceful, and efficient was the only way he could describe her movements. He remembered how she danced in his arms, and he knew he wanted nothing else than to spend a lifetime watching her.

He shook away the mood. There was no sense in dwelling on something that may not be. "What did the ladies brigade want?"

"It seems they've got more schemes up their sleeves," she said.

"Like what?"

"They found out that Evan may be coming home."

"And?"

"And they all met at my father's house to discuss the wedding."

"The wedding?" He could barely say the words.

She stopped brushing and put her forehead down on her horse. "I cannot believe it. They've been making me a wedding dress." She raised her head and looked at him with unreadable eyes. "They were so excited because they could finally show it to me and have me try it on."

"They made you a wedding gown?"

"Complete with satin and lace and hours of hand embroidery." She went back to brushing. "I swear I never asked them for a wedding gown. I never asked them for this farm. I never asked them for anything."

"They merely provided you with what they thought you wanted." He didn't sound as if he believed her. Maybe he didn't.

She turned to him and put her hands on her hips. "I didn't ask for this," she snapped. "They made me put on the dress."

"I bet you looked lovely."

"Sure, like Cinderella." She stuffed the brush into its holder and stormed out of the stall. "They didn't stop at the dress."

"They didn't?" He couldn't help it. He liked the way she looked when she was angry. Lightning seemed to flash out of her eyes. Passion flushed her cheeks. He wanted to ball up all the energy and direct it straight to him.

"They didn't," she said, and picked up a bucket of water and watered the horse. "They have the whole wedding planned. They are giving Evan two days and then the church is rented, the cake will be baked and the band will be tuned up."

"Two days? From when? Today?"

"No, thank goodness." She sat down on a nearby hay

bale, the empty bucket still clutched in her hands. "Two days from the day he arrives in town."

Trevor crossed his arms across his chest to keep from grabbing her, holding her against him until her distress disappeared. "That could be today."

She shot up. "I'm going to go in and make dinner now."

"I already made it," he said.

"You did?" She sounded amazed.

"I can cook when I have to. How do you think I stayed fed these past few years?"

"I'm sorry, I didn't mean any insult."

He raised an eyebrow. He didn't believe her.

"What did you fix?" she asked contritely.

"I made chili."

"Chili? What's that?"

"It's a dish I learned to make when I was in Texas."

"What's in it?"

Since she sounded truly interested he decided he would share the basics. "It's a hot soup. I make it with beans and meat and tomatoes and various spices. Then it simmers all day. The longer it cooks the better it tastes."

"Really? Sounds like stew."

"Oh, it's not stew," he said, and put his hand on the small of her back and guided her out of the barn toward the house. "I also put chili peppers in it among other things."

"Hmm, I've never had chili peppers. Are they sweet?"

"They can be. They can also be hot and spicy. I like a good bowl of spicy chili on a cool evening. It goes especially well with cornbread."

"I have a good recipe for that," she said. "I can whip us up some if you'd like."

"Sounds like together we can make a feast." The thought of what else they could do together was never far from his mind.

She stepped up on the porch and turned to him. "Are you excited about Evan returning?"

"Of course," he lied. "It's been too many years since I've seen my brother." He studied her. Her expression was grave and thoughtful. He couldn't help it—he reached down and lifted her chin up. "You look nervous. Why's that?"

Her lovely eyes looked up at him, touching his heart and soul. He had to grit his teeth to keep from holding her, soothing her.

"Eight years is a long time."

"Yes." He ran his gaze along her bottom lip. "My brother hasn't contacted you?"

"No."

"Don't you find that odd. I mean, if you two were so in love . . ."

She pulled away from him. "What do you want me to say, Trevor?" She crossed her arms across her chest and leaned against the back door. "What would make you happy? Are you looking to pity me? Then pity me, because I'm wrong either way. If I'm not your brother's fiancée, then I'm a liar and a cheat. I've stolen your family home right out from under you without so much as a how-do-you-do and worse, quite worse actually. If I'm not Evan's fiancée then I'm a fallen woman for having spent nearly two weeks out here alone with you." She jabbed him with a pointed finger. "Oh, but it gets better, doesn't it? I mean, if I am your brother's fiancée then I'm pitiful, aren't I? What kind of man asks a woman to marry him, then runs off for eight years without so much as a single letter."

"Maddie, I—"

"That's why they made me that dress," she continued without letting him speak. "Those ladies in town think I'm pitiful. They believe that I've sacrificed my whole life for a man who can't even remember where I live. Their idea of the right thing is to see me married. That's what they think I deserve."

"What do you think you deserve?"

She clamped her mouth shut and, closing her eyes,

banged the back of her head against the screen door. She opened her eyes and they shimmered. "I know one thing; I don't deserve any of this."

"No," he said and cupped her cheek in his hand. "You don't deserve any of this." She looked at him—her soul in her eyes—and it made his heart stop.

"What about you?" she asked.

The question echoed into his soul and he let go of her as if she were suddenly too hot to touch. He stepped back and shoved his hands in his pockets. "What do you mean?"

"What do you believe?"

"About you or about Evan?"

"About marriage. Do you think you'll ever fall in love and marry?"

"Maybe," he said and shrugged. "If the right girl came along."

"What's she like?"

"Who?"

"Your right girl?"

"Hmm." He opened the door as a way to put off the conversation. "She would have to be even tempered."

"Why?" she asked and walked inside.

"Because I tend to be high-handed," he replied honestly. "I think there'd be a real mess if she were too headstrong."

"I've been called headstrong a time or two."

"See?" he said. "If you have to marry one of us, then you picked the right brother. Evan is very easygoing."

"Unlike you."

"Unlike me." Right now, this minute, he wanted her so bad he had to be careful. It would be so easy to lie to her to convince her to marry him instead. But Trevor was nothing if not a man of integrity. No matter what he had done during the war, there were certain lines he just wouldn't cross. Stealing his brother's future wife was one of them.

* * *

Dinner was the best she ever had. The chili had been so spicy that she'd had to drink cold milk from the well house to cool her tongue. Trevor had laughed and told her she would get used to a little spice in her life.

She smiled at the reminder and glanced over her shoulder. He sat in the big chair next to the fireplace and played with his fiddle. The light from the fire flashed on his dark hair and sparkled in his eyes. His elegant fingers flew over the strings, plucking sweet sounds.

The image left her heart singing. He looked up at her and sent her a grin as he switched to a sprightly country tune. She realized then that she stood in the kitchen, towel in hand and stared at him. The tune was to tease her about staring and perhaps coax her into coming into the living room and dancing with him.

It struck her that this might be the last dance she ever had with Trevor. For tomorrow come what may, she was going to have to tell everyone the truth.

She raised her chin and smiled back. She raised an eyebrow at the challenge the fiddle rang out and placed the towel on the counter. Then she lifted her skirts and did a little jig right there in the kitchen.

It was her way of letting him know that she would dance but not come any closer. He stood up and motioned with his eyes that she should come into the living room, while his feet tapped the male part of the dance.

She shook her head, a smile on her lips, and teased him with a twirl of her skirts as her feet flashed in rhythm to his tune. He moved closer, weaving the footwork toward the edge of the living room. She countered by moving closer, and yet neither touched the threshold that divided them.

The pace of the dance picked up. Maddie laughed and swirled and jigged to her heart's content, ever conscious of the threshold. The emotion in Trevor's eyes made her stomach quiver and her knees weak. He stepped in perfect rhythm to the male part of the dance, while he encouraged her to cross the line and go to his side.

She refused. The devilish flash in his eyes made secret promises to her soul, but still she refused. Instead, she tread the narrow line, careful of her place.

They stood together so close that her skirts touched his pants and yet, neither crossed the line. Heat flashed between them. Silent promises flew through the air as Maddie's skin grew warm, her senses oddly alert.

He finished the song with a crescendo. They both stopped on their respective edges of the line that divided the rooms. Maddie could barely breathe, and found herself intrigued by the pounding of his pulse at the base of his neck, where his shirt hung open.

"Maddie," he said in a whisper, drawing her attention to his face. He was a breath away. She knew then that she had to kiss him. Her soul screamed for his touch. Nothing else mattered but this moment. This breath. This kiss.

She rose up on tiptoes and touched her mouth to his. The heat of his mouth shot through her. His arms went around her, drawing her over the threshold and into his arms. She explored the hunger inside her. The kiss was filled with longing and a need she never knew she had.

He ran his hands down her back, spanned her waist and clasped her to his heart. She loved every minute of it. The taste, the touch, the lightning that went through her. She knew that no matter what happened tomorrow it would all be worth it because of this one kiss.

He pulled away and ran his hand over her hair, cupping her cheek. "Maddie, Maddie."

Her hands were pressed to his chest. She tested the hard muscle of him then buried her face in the spot where his shoulder and neck met. He smelled so good, like her soap, man, and home.

They stood there a long moment and she knew that as much as she wanted the moment to last forever, it could not. There was simply too much between them. Tears welled up at the back of her eyes. There was so much she needed to tell him.

She looked up to find him watching her with such tenderness that it broke her heart. How could she admit the truth and yet, how could she lie? She took a step back, breaking the contact and he let her go.

She fought her way over to the counter and braced herself against the sink. "Trevor."

"Maddie."

"Trevor, I'm sorry—"

Some odd emotion came over him as if he didn't want to hear what she had to say. She clutched the sink.

"No, Maddie," he said. "I'm the one who is sorry. I'll move into town in the morning."

"No!" she said quickly. "No. I have already made arrangements to move back to my father's house. This is your house Trevor. It's not right that I'm here." She pulled a folded paper out of the pocket of her apron and handed it to him. "Here, here is the deed. I had the county put it back in your name."

He took the paper from her. Their fingers touched briefly and she gasped and moved to her bedroom door. Her fingers clutched the door knob. "I'm sorry." It was all she could get out. The rest would have to come in the morning. She slipped into her bedroom and closed the door behind her. She turned the lock with a smart click then flung herself on the bed.

She was in love with him. The horror of that truth hit her. She was in love with Trevor Montgomery, and after the truth came out he would never want to look at her again.

Chapter Ten

Maddie didn't sleep a wink. Up by 5 A.M., she splashed cold water on her tired eyes and stared at her reflection in the tiny mirror above the dresser.

Everything had gone so terribly wrong.

She had fallen in love with Trevor, the one man whom she could never marry. Even if she didn't tell the truth, she would become his brother's wife. Once she told the truth he would lose all respect for her. All because of a silly story Robert made up two whole years ago.

Somehow, some way, the story had taken up a life of its own. Her thoughts went to Mrs. Addlestone and all the ladies who had worked so hard for so many years. It hurt her to think how upset they would be. How broken-hearted.

Why, the news that she had made the whole thing up could even end up killing the older ladies. Maddie winced at the idea. Then she thought of her father's reaction. He would be so angry and so disappointed. She would be marked a fallen woman. Heck, even Stuart wouldn't be able to look at her again without knowing what she was.

She splashed more water on her face and wiped it dry. Cross that bridge when you come to it, Maddie told herself.

It was one of her mother's favorite sayings. It was how Maddie had gotten through her mother's death.

Right now she had chores to do. The animals needed to be fed and the cow milked. Then true to her word, she would move back home. She glanced at the small trunk she had spent the night packing. She really didn't have much that was hers and that was fine. Wyoming was looking pretty good right now, and if she went she wouldn't be able to take much.

Maddie felt better now that she had come to a decision. It was good to finally be in control of her life again. She dressed quickly; brushed and braided her hair into a long braid that ran down her back.

Satisfied that she looked presentable, Maddie walked out into the kitchen. The house was quiet in the early morning. Trevor would not admit it but he was still recovering. She could tell because he went to bed early and got up after seven. She knew it wasn't laziness that kept him in bed. When he was up he was working. Whether he was cutting wood, repairing something or walking the farm, he was always going.

Her father would say Trevor was driven. It was clear something drove him to keep going even when his body wanted to rest. Maddie made it a point to remind him to slow down whenever she saw that he was out of breath. Goodness, she would miss him. Miss seeing him come around a corner, his broad shoulders and quick smile lightening her mood.

She grabbed her oldest jacket, buttoned it tight against the early morning cold, put on work gloves and stepped outside. The chill took her breath away. But it was the silence that attracted her.

In the dark of a fall morning, the chickens still roosted, the birds no longer called to claim their territory. Even the gentle hum of insects was gone. The frost killed off those that didn't hibernate.

In the quiet of fall and winter, Maddie could look up at the stars and marvel. There were so many of them and they seemed so serene so far from her silly problems.

She blew out a breath. It clouded her vision, reminding her that winter was just around the bend. When she left, she would leave all this. The woods, the animals, the storehouse of food she had spent the summer preserving.

She shook off the loneliness that followed that thought and went to the barn. Inside it was dark and warm. She lit a lamp and hung it near the stall. Then she went to work, hauling water and hay to the cow and the two horses. She worked steadily for fifteen minutes or so. Her mind on what she would take when she left, what she would leave.

"You must be Evan's gal."

The sound of a strange man's voice was the last thing she ever expected to hear in the barn. Startled, Maddie turned to face the intruder. "What?!"

A tall thin man leaned lazily against the post across from where she worked. He wore a flannel shirt, suspenders, a pair of wool slacks and a six shooter on both hips. "Who are you and what are you doing in my barn?" she demanded. Her mind scurried to find a weapon.

When she had first come to the farm, she carried a rifle with her everywhere until she became comfortable with living alone. Then she rarely brought a gun with her. Now that Trevor was here she always left the guns in the house. Maddie clutched the bucket in front of her and tried to remember where she put the pitchfork. "I asked you a question."

"Spunky thing," he said and narrowed his eyes at her. His gaze went from the top of her head to her feet and back, ignoring the bucket and lingering on her bosom. "Not Evan's usual type."

"If you don't tell me who you are right now, I will scream," she said. She spied the pitchfork off to her right. "I have a healthy scream. It'll carry to the house."

"Go ahead," he said when he saw her glance at the pitch-fork. "I like a woman with fight in her."

"I'm leaving." Maddie said and raised her chin. She decided it was best to treat him like a mad dog. Move slowly but surely away from him. If she didn't make any sudden moves, perhaps he wouldn't either.

She eased along her side of the barn toward the door. He grinned and watched her go. Maddie's heart raced in her chest. Her knuckles were white as she clutched the bucket.

"I don't know where you think you're going," he said and a click brought her gaze to his hand. He had drawn a gun and cocked it in one smooth motion.

Maddie froze in place. By choosing to move toward the door, she had moved away from the pitchfork. There was nothing left to do but turn and face the man head on. "You still haven't told me who you are and what you think you're doing?"

"I'm a friend of Evan's," he said and stepped toward her. "He has something of mine and I want it back." He stopped a few inches from her, his eyes gleaming with something that made her stomach lurch.

"Evan isn't here."

"That's what they told me in town, but I'm not believing it. I have it on good authority that he's coming back this way."

"Evan hasn't been here for eight years. What makes you think he's coming home now?"

"I'd have come home a long time ago if I had a feisty little thing like you waiting for me." He ran the barrel of his gun along her upper arm. His gaze darkened. "Maybe I don't need Evan to come home. Maybe I can trade what he owes me for a little bit of fun with you."

He leered at her and Maddie panicked. She swung the bucket up hard, knocking the gun away. At the same time she kicked him where her brothers told her it would down a man. He let out an oath, bent in half and Maddie scrambled for the door.

She flung it open and raced toward the house. "Trevor!" she yelled at the top of her lungs. But she wasn't fast enough. The stranger grabbed her by her hair and yanked her back. She stumbled and struggled not to fall. "Trevor!" she screamed over and over.

She fought the man. He cuffed her, sending her flying toward the cold, hardened ground. The impact pushed all the air out of her lungs, leaving her dazed. She was pulled to her feet. He wrapped his arm around her neck and held her against his wiry body. She felt the cold steel of a gun barrel pressed against her temple.

"Don't even think about it," the stranger snarled. Maddie's vision cleared slowly. She saw Trevor standing in the doorway dressed only in pants, suspenders hanging at the sides. His chest and feet were bare and exposed to the cold air.

"Trevor," Maddie whispered. In the craziness of the situation all she could think about was that Trevor was going to relapse if he didn't go inside where it was warm.

The stranger tightened his hold on her. "Put down the gun, Montgomery or I will shoot her."

Trevor's heart banged against his chest but his head was incredibly clear. A long, lean, mean-looking gunfighter stood not ten feet from the cabin and he had a gun to Maddie's head. Trevor had all he could do not to beat the man to a pulp.

"Put the rifle down," the man ordered.

Trevor realized he had a gun trained to the man's head. He was a good shot. Good enough to take the stranger out and leave Maddie standing. But if he did then she would see him, as he really was . . . a ruthless killer.

"Let the girl go," Trevor said. He kept his tone a simple but deadly drawl.

"You shoot and she dies." He cocked the gun he held on Maddie.

Trevor could see the anger growing on Maddie's face. She fisted her hands and Trevor felt terror. "Maddie, no."

It was too late. Maddie put one hand over the other and drove her elbow into the man's gut. He yelped in surprise and the gun momentarily pushed away. Maddie ducked and Trevor took the shot.

A second shot rang out less than a heartbeat later. Trevor ran toward them. The sharp scent of gunsmoke filled the air. Maddie met him halfway. He grabbed her and held her as if he would never let her go.

She clung to his waist and he pushed her behind him.

He cocked his rifle and pointed it where the stranger lay.

A pool of blood seeped around the man's body. His six shooter sat on the ground just out of reach. Trevor had his free arm around Maddie's waist. "Are you okay?"

"I think so."

"We need to get you inside," they said in unison. Trevor shook his head. He'd ask her why she said it later. Right now it was enough that she agreed with him. He kept his body between her and the man and eased her backward onto the porch. The man didn't move. Trevor figured he was dead, but with Maddie still outside, he wasn't going to take even a slight chance.

They got into the house and Trevor slammed the thick wooden door closed and threw the bolt. He gathered Maddie into his arms and coddled her against his heart. She buried her head in his shoulder and shook like a leaf.

Heart still racing, Trevor could do nothing but cling to her. Her screams had awakened him out of a dead sleep. He'd come out of the house at a rush and stopped dead when he saw the man cuff her, then yank her against him.

Trevor had seen red. He'd cocked the rifle and the sound brought the man's head up. It was then that he put the gun to Maddie's temple and Trevor had stopped cold.

She was safe now he thought, and buried his face in her hair. She smelled like fall air and warm woman. "Madeline," he whispered raggedly. "Madeline."

She lifted her tear-stained face to his and he kissed her. It was an unforgiving kiss, a meeting of souls, desperate, joyous. Her mouth was soft and warm and wet. Her skin smelled sweet. He wanted to snatch her up and take her to his bed, to claim her as his.

"Trevor," she whispered against his mouth. It was both heaven and hell. Her hands caressed his face. "I—"

He didn't give her time to speak. He dove back into the kiss, drawing her close. What he wanted more than anything was to make her his. It was a losing battle. She belonged to Evan.

He softened the kiss, leaving small kisses on her face, her cheeks, her temple. It took all his strength. "Shh," he said and kissed her forehead. "Shh. It's okay. You're safe now."

"Trevor."

Before she could kiss him again, he drew her against his bare chest. He knew she could feel the galloping of his heart, but it was sweet torture to have her cheek against his bare skin. It was the closest he would ever get to holding her.

He leaned against the door and took a few deep breaths. He had to get control of the situation. She was an innocent. If anything happened it would be on his head and he had enough to beat himself up with. He didn't need seducing his brother's fiancée on the list.

"Madeline," he said when he had control of himself. "What happened out there?"

"He was in the barn," she said. "He said Evan owed him something. Then he said I could pay up." She clung tighter to him. He could feel the tears rolling down her cheeks, wetting his skin. He ran a hand soothingly down her back.

Inside he wanted to take the man apart inch by inch. "Did he hurt you?"

"I smashed him with a bucket and ran. All I could think of was to call for you."

"It's okay," he said softly. "You're safe. We're safe."

"You killed him."

Her words caused him to flinch. "I believe so."

She gazed up at him, her expression wary. "You've killed before."

"Yes." It was all he could say. She knew the truth now. He was a cold-blooded killer.

She reached up and soothed his cheek with her hand. "It's okay," she said.

"It's never okay to kill a man," he said. She was soft and warm against him and yet he could feel the cold doors around his heart closing. It was his only protection against the pain reality caused. Reality would come around sooner than later and she would step away from him in horror.

"Sometimes you have to do what you have to do," she said. "This time you had to shoot him. He was capable of killing me."

"Yes, he was."

"But still it hurts you."

He didn't say anything. She blew out a breath and pressed her cheek to his chest and hugged him close. "It hurts you, yet you didn't think twice about doing it."

"You were in danger."

"I owe you my life." The gratitude in her voice slashed at his heart. He didn't want her gratitude. He didn't want her pity either. He pushed her away.

"I need to check on the man. I want you to stay inside."

She hugged her waist and studied him with a brave tear-stained face. "What if he's not dead?"

"He won't hurt you. I promise you that. Now, lock the door behind me."

She nodded her agreement. Trevor checked his rifle and moved to the door. "Wait!"

He stopped, his hand hovering on the door knob. He turned to see her taking his great coat off the coat tree.

"Put this on," she said. "The last thing we need is for you to survive this gunfight only to catch your death of cold."

Something inside him broke. Even though she knew he was a killer she still cared enough to see that he was warm and dry. He took the coat from her, reached down and wrapped his arm around her waist. Then he kissed her hard on the mouth. Before she could say a word, he let her go, threw on the coat and walked out the door.

Maddie wrapped her arms around her waist and stared at the door. He kissed her again and she had kissed him back. There had been nothing tender about it. The kiss had been an expression of desperation, fear, joy, and love.

Maddie touched her slightly swollen lips. She loved Trevor. She knew it deep in her heart. It had nothing to do with this house, the farm, or the town's expectations. She wanted Trevor. She wanted to hold him next to her heart, lean on him when she was afraid, take care of him when he was sick. She hugged her waist tighter. She wanted to have little boys with black hair and quicksilver eyes. And she was willing to give up her freedom to make it happen.

Maddie swallowed hard and went to the window. She looked out to see Trevor crouched down beside the stranger. He had taken one shot and brought the man down. One shot. Trevor was not a stranger to guns. It was clear he could protect his own.

He picked up the man's guns and tucked them away. Then he picked the big stranger up and carried him toward the barn. Curious, Maddie opened the door and ran out.

"Trevor?"

"He's not dead. I'm going to take him into town and let Doc look at him."

Maddie turned and went back into the house. She grabbed an undershirt and a warm wool shirt for Trevor and an old blanket for the wounded man. Then she ran back out to the barn. Trevor had put the stranger in the back of the wagon. He brought her mare out and hitched her to the vehicle.

"What are you doing?" Trevor asked when he spotted Maddie.

She handed him his clothes. "You need to be dressed if we're going into town. The blanket is for the wounded. It helps with the shock."

He took the shirts from her. "We're not going into town. You are staying here."

"Don't be silly," she replied and walked away from him. "I have to go with you to tell the sheriff what happened." She got up in the wagon and tucked the blanket around the unconscious man. "Why isn't he conscious?"

"He hit his head on a rock when he went down."

Maddie glanced over and saw that Trevor had taken off his coat. He had turned his well-muscled back to her. Maddie let her eyes feast on him. His skin was a golden tan. It was clear he had been out in the sun. She wondered what he had done since the war.

He tossed his undershirt on, stuffed his arms in the wool shirt and pulled it over his head. She glanced away when he turned. "Do you think he'll live?"

Trevor stepped over next to her. "The bullet went through his shoulder and he's lost a lot of blood. We have to get him into town right away."

"I can press on the wound and try to keep him from bleeding more."

"I won't ask that of you," Trevor said. He shrugged back into the coat.

"He'll lose too much blood if someone doesn't keep pressure on the wound."

"He could wake up," Trevor said and jumped up in the back of the wagon. "I'm not going to take that chance." He checked the man's shoulder. Maddie saw that Trevor had pulled off the man's shirt and wadded it up over the wound.

"Then I'll drive," she said.

Trevor looked at her. He stopped everything, his gaze filling with concern and anger. "He hurt you." He reached out and touched her cheek and she winced at the pain his touch caused. "I'm sorry."

"It's okay." Maddie touched her cheek gingerly. "How bad is it?"

"Pretty bad," Trevor said. He looked like he wanted to smash something.

She put her hand on his. "It's okay. I'll get a compress on it once we get into town. Now, you press on the wound and I'll drive."

He frowned at her. "You are headstrong, aren't you?"

"I told you I was," she said with a quick smile and a wince at the pain the smile cost her. "No," she said when he moved to touch her. "If he becomes conscious, you'll need to restrain him."

She stepped over the prone man and hopped out of the wagon. "Besides, Betsy is used to my driving. She might act up if a stranger was at the reins."

"Don't tell me," he said as he settled in. "Your mare is as headstrong as you are."

"Yes, she is," Maddie said, and climbed into the driver's seat. "That's why we get along so well. We understand each other."

Maddie settled in and snapped the reins. The ride into town only took ten minutes, but she knew the man in the back might not have that long to live. She glanced at Trevor's dark head. It was clear he carried a lot of guilt on his shoulders. She didn't want this episode to add to his grief.

They were in town just before 7 A.M. Doc Emerson had been in the middle of breakfast when they knocked on his door. He and Trevor picked up the wounded man and carried him into the surgeon's room.

Mrs. Emerson gasped at the sight of Maddie's face. Maddie touched her cheek and realized it had swollen. She let the elderly woman push her into a kitchen chair. "Sit, let me take care of that for you."

Mrs. Emerson was small and compact. Her gray hair was in twin braids which wrapped around her head like a crown. She wore a plain linen blouse and a pretty blue calico skirt. Over it was a thick white apron, which tied around the woman's waist. She fussed with water and a cloth, and brought it to Maddie. "Here, put this on your cheek."

The cloth was cold and wet. Maddie did as she was told, wincing at the pain the simple pressure caused.

"You'll be lucky if your eye doesn't swell shut," Mrs. Emerson declared, and sat down in a chair across from Maddie. "Tell me what happened."

The door to the surgery room opened and Trevor walked out. "I'm going to get the sheriff." He came over and hunkered down beside Maddie. "Are you okay?"

The concern in his eyes made her want to lean into his shoulder and cry. She bit back the emotion. "Mrs. Emerson is taking good care of me."

"I'll send word to your family," Trevor said. He stood and squeezed her shoulder. "You're an amazing woman, Madeline Morgan."

She held in the sigh until he walked out the door. Then she let it out slow and sweet. Mrs. Emerson patted Maddie's knee. "It's like that is it?"

Horrified, Maddie glanced at the older woman's knowing gaze. "I beg your pardon?"

"You're in love with him."

Maddie was speechless. "Well . . . I . . ."

"It's okay," Mrs. Emerson said and patted Maddie's knee again. "I'm good with secrets."

Maddie broke down then. Tears sprang to her eyes and she slumped in the chair. "It's so complicated."

"It always is," the older woman said, and gently took the cloth from Maddie. She went to the sink and rinsed it with fresh water and handed it back. "Here, put this over your eyes too."

"You don't understand," Maddie said and did what she was told. "The whole town thinks I'm in love with his brother. Even Trevor thinks that."

"Well now, that does sound like a complication."

"I can't tell the truth. I've been taking care of Trevor alone for two weeks. That was one thing while I was Evan's fiancée. It will be quite another if I wasn't. Why the shock might even kill Mrs. Addlestone."

"That old biddy can take a lot. In fact, I'm convinced she'll still be round when I'm long gone."

"They made me a wedding gown," Maddie blurted. "They are so excited about my impending marriage that they have the whole affair planned right down to the pot luck after."

"So, to keep the town happy, you'll marry a man you don't love."

Maddie bit her lip. "I hope it doesn't go that far."

"What if it does?"

"Then it's nothing more than I deserve for allowing the lie to grow." Maddie shook her head, pulled the cloth off her face and looked at the older woman with the gently disapproving eyes. "I'll just have to dedicate my life to making Evan happy."

"What about you, Maddie? Don't you deserve to be happy?"

"I'm not so sure anymore."

Chapter Eleven

The stranger died in the doctor's office. The sheriff made a report and the undertaker came in to remove the body. Maddie's family came for her and took her home. Her face was swollen and badly bruised. Maddie's brothers Henry and Jack took one look at Maddie's bruise and grimly thanked Trevor for seeing that the man didn't survive.

Trevor sat in the saloon. It seemed like the perfect place for a cold-blooded killer to be in the middle of the afternoon. He nursed a glass of bad whiskey and wondered what it was that Evan owed the man. What had Evan done these past few years to bring on the likes of the lean gunfighter?

His thoughts turned to Maddie and the kiss they had shared this morning. Damn, he wanted her. If he were to be honest, he wanted it all; Maddie, the farm, children. It would never happen. Even if she didn't belong to his brother, she would never want to settle down with a man who had killed more men than he could count.

The saloon doors opened and closed. Trevor hunkered down over his drink. He didn't want to talk to anyone. Right now he wanted to lose himself in his drink.

"What can I get you?" the bartender asked when another man eased up to the bar.

"I'll take a draft of your best beer," the man said. Trevor frowned at the sound of that voice. It was strangely familiar. He turned his head.

The man standing next to the bar was the same height and build as Trevor, perhaps a bit leaner in the shoulders. He wore a hat low over his eyes. His duster was gray with road dirt, his hands encased in leather gloves. The bartender drew the draft and passed it to the stranger. He pushed the hat off his head to reveal black hair. It was thick and shaggy and Trevor's heart lurched.

"Hello, Evan."

His brother turned and looked at him. He squinted pale blue eyes and stared. "Trevor? My gosh, Trevor!" Evan grinned his devilish smile and grabbed Trevor into a giant bear hug. "I didn't know you were back home. How long have you been back?"

"I've been back a little over a month," Trevor said. He hugged his brother back and stepped out of the embrace. "We were expecting you."

"We?" Evan asked and took a swallow of his beer. He wiped his hand over his mouth.

"We, meaning myself, Madeline and the whole town."

"Madeline who?" Evan squinted at him and grinned. "You got yourself a gal?"

"No, she's not my gal," Trevor said, his tone more of a snarl than it should have been. "Madeline Morgan, your fiancée."

"My fiancée?"

"Yes. You were seeing her steady before you left for the war. It seems you asked her to marry you and she has spent the past eight years waiting for you to come home."

"Madeline Morgan," Evan said thoughtfully. He took another drink of his beer. "Now, I remember Robert Morgan. Went to school with him, but heck there were a lot of girls back then." He took another swallow. "I suppose I'll remember her when I see her."

Trevor tried to hide his disgust. Evan hadn't changed a bit. He always was free and easy with the girls. Trevor wondered how many women were sitting at home right now, waiting for Evan to come back as promised. "Why'd you come back to Boltonville?"

Evan shrugged. "I figured it was time." He scratched his head. "Eight years is a long time to be on the road. Heard you were doing the same thing, big brother."

"I made it home for Ma's funeral."

"Yeah, I heard about that. I tried to make it home too, but got waylaid in Chicago. If I remember right, there was a poker game and a fight broke out. By the time I could ride again it had been a month." He shrugged. "I figured it wasn't worth coming back for after that long a time."

"Have you stopped by the farm?"

"Naw, I figured I'd have a drink first. Fortify myself as it were." Evan brightened. "But hey, you've been home over a month. The old place can't look too bad, now can it?"

"The place looks great," Trevor said and tossed down his drink. "Madeline's kept it up."

"Who?"

"Madeline Morgan," Trevor said through gritted teeth. He really wanted to plant his fist in his brother's face. Here he had the most wonderful woman in the world and he didn't even remember her name. "The ladies in town found out that Madeline was waiting for your return, so they got together and passed around a petition. Seems everyone had had enough of the farm being left to rot. So they had the mayor declare that it belonged to Madeline."

"Why would they do that?"

"Since you were engaged to Madeline, they figured you would marry her when you got back."

"So they didn't really give away the farm. She was just holding it in trust or something."

"Yeah," Trevor said and signaled for another whiskey. "Or something."

"So, did Madeline take good care of the place?"

"Yeah, it looks like it did before Ma died."

Evan swallowed the rest of his beer and wiped his mouth with the back of his hand. "Sounds fortuitous to me," Evan said, his grin widening. "I usually have good taste in women. What's she look like?"

"She's beautiful, charming, and a handful," Trevor said, and swallowed half his whiskey in one gulp. He waited for the burn to reach down his throat and numb the pain near his heart. It didn't. "She's something. One look and you don't know if you want to kiss her or arm-wrestle her? Anyway, she gets under your skin real fast."

"Beautiful and from the sounds of it, smart," Evan said and slapped him on the back. "I knew I could pick them. I swear brother, when your luck's on a run, it's on a run. Come on let's go get a look at my soon-to-be wife."

"Wait." Trevor grabbed his brother's hand and pushed it away. "There was trouble this morning. That's why we were expecting you."

Evan crossed his arms over his chest and sobered. "What kind of trouble?"

"Seems a friend of yours came looking for you."

"A friend?"

"Someone said he called himself Angel," Trevor said. "He said you owed him something."

"I didn't owe that snaked-eye mongrel anything," Evan spit out. "Where is he?"

"He's dead."

"Dead? What happened?"

"He came around the farm looking for you. Seems he took one look at Madeline and decided if you weren't home, then he'd take out what you owed him on your gal."

"Whoa," Evan said and grabbed Trevor's forearm. "I told you I didn't owe him a thing."

"He thought so. Enough that he grabbed Madeline. She fought back so he cuffed her."

"She kill him?"

Trevor shook his head. "I killed him."

"Good. I owe you."

"You don't owe me anything," Trevor said with disgust. "Except maybe an explanation. How the heck did you know this guy, and why did he know you were coming back to Boltonville?"

Evan blew out a breath and leaned against the bar. "It's a bit of a story."

"I'm not going anywhere."

"Then I need another beer," Evan waved at the bartender. "Barkeep." He motioned at his empty glass.

Trevor waited patiently while his brother swallowed half his new drink and wiped his mouth with the back of his hand. "Well?"

"Well, I discovered early on that military life wasn't exactly for me."

Trevor tried not to think about all the young boys who had gone off to war. It seemed so romantic and heroic. It wasn't.

"Don't get me wrong," Evan said. "The uniform was sharp looking and it got the ladies' attention."

"Bartender, bring me another whiskey." Trevor knew he was going to need something if he had to hear one more time how his little brother got all the girls. Somehow, in his heart of hearts he had hoped that if Evan came back he'd have lost his charm. From the looks of his brother, that hadn't happened. Evan knew how to make any gal fall in love with him.

"Anyway," Evan continued, "I didn't have the heart to actually shoot at a man. So when Ma died, I used that as a reason to take some leave. But like I said, I got waylaid in Chicago." He took another swig of his beer. "I never went back."

"You were AWOL?"

"Oh, I was on leave. Just the permanent sort."

"What did you do?"

"I figured I couldn't come back home. The unit would be able to track me down too easy. So I stayed in Chicago for a while. Found me a real sweet gal who let me stay at her place. I made a good living gambling."

"You didn't return to the war?"

Evan shrugged. "I didn't have the stomach for it."

"Where'd you meet Angel?"

"I played him one night. He lost a lot of money and got mad." Evan took another pull of his beer. "He claimed I cheated."

"Did you?"

"Naw. There was never any need to cheat. Anyway, there was a fight. Things got nasty. Angel had his gang bust into my gal's place. They messed her up bad. It wasn't safe so I lit out of town."

"What about the girl?"

"I sent her all the cash I had. It wasn't enough to make up for what they did to her face. But I figured it was better than a stick in the eye. I heard later on that she found herself a fisherman and got married." He shrugged. "She had a body on her that wouldn't quit."

"You didn't love her."

"She didn't love me either. We had a few good times and that was enough."

Trevor tossed the rest of the whiskey down his throat. He loved his brother. He was his brother after all, but that didn't mean he had to like the way Evan treated women.

"So, I'm all cashed out and I found myself a group of drifters. The war was over and we went out west, punched some cattle for a while. That got old or maybe I got old. I'm not much suited for sleeping on the ground. So, I figured I'd come home. See what the old homestead looked like. Collect some of my things. I'd plum forgotten that there was a gal here in town waiting on me."

"I don't know how anyone could forget Madeline?"

Evan grinned and slapped Trevor on the back. "She must be something. Tell you what, let's go on down to the barber and get cleaned up. Then I'm thinking I need to pay my gal a visit."

"Let me ask you one more thing before we go."

"Sure, shoot."

"Are there any more like Angel coming after you? I think Madeline needs to know if there are. She was pretty shaken up today."

"I think Angel was the last of them. It's hard to tell though, when a man gets a burr in his saddle it doesn't matter what you do. If he wants to come after you, he comes after you."

Trevor ground his teeth at the thought. It was clear his brother's devil-may-care attitude hadn't changed in all the years he'd been gone. Maybe Trevor wouldn't leave town when they got married. Maybe he needed to stick around and keep an eye on the homestead, keep an eye on Madeline. It might kill him to do so, but he couldn't abandon her, not now, not ever. Somewhere along the way he had fallen in love with her.

"You'll never guess who's at the barber's right now getting a bath and a shave," Henry said as he burst into the parlor.

Beth stood up, caught up in her brother's enthusiasm. "Is it the governor?"

"Nope."

"Mayor's son?"

"Nope." Henry grinned at Maddie. "Someone who's been gone a long time."

It felt like a bolt of lightning ran down Maddie's back. She stood straight up. "Evan Montgomery."

"Yep," Henry said, his expression excited. "I saw him myself. He and Trevor came in and paid for a bath and a shave. They were talking too."

"They were?" Beth said, egging her brother on. "Who were they talking about?"

"Who do you think?" Henry said. "I'm going to go tell Papa."

Maddie's legs gave out from under her and she sat down on the settee with a whoosh.

"Maddie," Amelia said and put down her book. "How wonderful. Your prince has come home."

"What a day to do it," Beth said and came over to sit beside Maddie. "Look at your face. Why, it's all swollen and hideous."

"Beth!" Amelia gasped.

"Well, it's true," Beth said and took Maddie's hand. She patted it. "Too bad he couldn't have come in yesterday when you were wearing the gown. You looked like a princess then."

Maddie felt like all the air had left the room. Her hands had grown numb, her heart raced. Her sisters' voices dimmed and she knew the day of reckoning had come. Evan was home and he was talking to Trevor. She stood up energized by horror.

Now Trevor would find out the truth. Evan had never courted her. Evan didn't love her, and she had no right to the place she had established in the community. She was a liar and worse, she was an opportunist. Trevor would never look at her the same again.

"Maddie, it's okay, you don't look that bad," Amelia said and took Maddie's hand. "Come on, let's fix up your hair and put some powder on your cheek. You'll see. You'll look pretty as a picture when Evan gets here."

"When Evan gets here?" Maddie echoed, panic rising in her throat. Oh my, what would she do if he came to the door?

Amelia pulled her toward the stairs. Papa came out of his study, his eyes filled with concern. "Madeline, are you all right?"

"Papa, I—"

There was a knock at the door. Everyone whirled and stared at it. Maddie stopped breathing. The knock came again and Mrs. Poole came out of the kitchen.

"Aren't you going to answer that?" she asked and bustled past the stunned family members. She opened the door to find Mrs. Selis and Mrs. Lance standing in the doorway.

Maddie drew in a deep breath. For a horrified moment she thought it was the Montgomerys. "Good afternoon, everyone," Mrs. Selis said as she stepped into the foyer. "Robert, how wonderful to see you." She passed the girls and held out her hand to Papa.

Papa sent her a wry grin and kissed her hand. "Blanche, what brings you here in the middle of the afternoon?"

"Why, we heard the news and had to come tell Maddie ourselves," Mrs. Lance said. "Evan's in town. He's at the barber's right now, bathing and shaving. It's our bet your house will be the first place he comes once he's cleaned up."

Maddie wanted to argue the point, but one glance at her father made her think better of it.

"My, my, look at you, dear," Mrs. Selis said. "What happened to your face? Amelia, see that your sister looks the best she can." The older woman smiled at Papa. "It takes a woman's touch to see that these things go off without a hitch. I hope you don't mind."

"No, of course not," Papa said with a dazed look.

Maddie went over and kissed her father on the cheek. Then she whispered in his ear. "Be careful Papa. Mrs. Selis hopes you're next."

At which point her father turned beet red and blustered something under his breath.

"Whatever did he say?" Mrs. Selis asked.

"He said he had to go into town on business," Maddie said, as she watched her father retreat from the situation. "Mrs. Poole, please see that our guests have a fresh pot of tea. I think there are some of those cookies left over from yesterday." Then she smiled wickedly at the older women and took Amelia's arm. "Come on Amelia, let's go upstairs where you can work magic on me."

Maddie climbed the stairs dragging her middle sister along. She glanced over her shoulder at Beth. "Beth, would you be so kind as to entertain our guests?"

Beth smiled. "Of course." She held out her hand and pointed toward the parlor. "Ladies, please do come in and sit down."

Maddie pulled Amelia up the stairs and into the first room on the right. There were four bedrooms upstairs. One for her parents, one for the girls, and one for the boys. The fourth had been turned into a hobby room. It was where the girls sewed and painted, and where the boys worked on woodworking and played chess.

In effect it was a nursery, now grown too small for the occupants. Amelia closed the door of the girls' bedroom. It was stark but cozy, with two small beds and a mirrored vanity where the girls did their hair. Maddie hadn't slept in this room in two years and it showed. Right now, Papa had set her up with a cot in the hobby room.

"Maddie, are you all right?" Amelia asked. She leaned against the door and studied Maddie. Maddie blew out a breath. Amelia may be a bookworm, but she was very astute at reading people.

"No," Maddie said and paced the room.

"Is it because Evan is back? Don't worry, I can help you look wonderful." She picked up a brush and a blue velvet hair ribbon. "He'll fall in love all over again when he sees you."

"That's the problem," Maddie said as she paced. "He never loved me in the first place."

"What?"

"I said he never loved me in the first place."

"But you said you were engaged . . ."

"I never said anything. Robert made the whole story up to keep the suitors off my back."

"Robert made the story up? I don't understand."

"Of course you wouldn't understand," Maddie said, trying not to wail. "You had your nose in a book, while Beth ran around flirting with everything in pants. That's why Papa said I had to marry first. He had to have some way of keeping the men away from Beth."

"Why didn't you take your time and find a good man?"

"I couldn't. The Schyler boys thought of the grand idea of pooling their money and creating a pot that would go to the man who married me. Soon, every single man who needed money was knocking at the door, even Rudy Harrison."

"Doesn't Rudy live for the saloon?"

"He had a particularly large bar tab that month."

"Oh, no."

"Oh, Beth, I couldn't even walk down the street to Susie's without being accosted by men with missing teeth, greasy hair, or dirt still under their fingernails." Maddie stopped short. "Then Mr. Smitherton stopped by."

"Mr. Smitherton? Old man Smitherton? Isn't he ninety?"

"I believe he's eighty-five," Maddie said. "I was actually to a point where I considered him. I mean, how long can a man actually live? But then he smiled that toothless smile and breathed his nasty breath and I knew I just couldn't."

"So Robert came to your rescue."

"Yes," Maddie said, and sat down on her sister's bed. "Dear Robert, who is currently in Wyoming Territory. He started the rumor and the ladies picked it up from there. I tried to deny the whole thing, but you see how Mrs. Selis and Mrs. Lance can be. No one listened."

Amelia sat down beside Maddie and put her arm around her sister. "And now the whole town expects a wedding."

"If I tell the truth now, why, then people will believe the worst, what with me living out there alone with Trevor for weeks." She glanced at her sister. "He was sick and Doc Emerson said at the very least, I owed him for housing me for the past two years. So, I stayed and nursed him. Nothing happened Amelia." Maddie bit her bottom lip. "Well, almost nothing."

"Almost nothing?"

"I kissed him," she whispered.

"Who?"

"Trevor."

"Maddie!"

"I think . . . no, I know I'm in love with him."

"Oh, Maddie! How did this happen?"

"I don't know," she said and wrung her hands. "It just did. What am I going to do—everyone thinks I'm going to marry Evan."

"Well, shoot. What did Trevor say when you told him?"

"I didn't tell him," Maddie said sheepishly.

"Madeline Morgan. You've been living alone with him for three weeks and you never told him the truth?"

"I planned on it. I did, but then it never seemed like the right time."

"So, he doesn't even know how you feel?"

"How could I tell him I have feelings for him when he thinks I'm in love with his brother?"

"Now Evan is back," Amelia said. "They must both have figured out that they were duped."

Maddie covered her face with her hands. "What am I going to do?" Pain sliced through her. "Trevor will never look at me the same way." She looked at her sister. "Not to mention what Papa will do."

"But you can't keep up the lie now. Surely Evan is telling everyone the truth."

Maddie swallowed hard. "The ladies made me that beautiful dress. They have the whole wedding planned." She shook her head. "I've shamed the family."

Amelia took a deep breath and let it out slow. "This is all Papa's fault."

"What?"

"This is all Papa's fault," Amelia concluded. "If he hadn't used you to slow Beth down, then you wouldn't have had to resort to making up this story. To think, Mr. Smitherton had come calling." She shook her head. "How did you stand it?"

Maddie lifted her head. "You're right. This is Papa's fault. He used me to keep Beth in line." She stood up, righteous indignation filling her. "I need to go downstairs and have a talk with him."

"Just one thing," Amelia said.

"What?"

"Aren't you even a little bit curious to see what Evan looks like? I mean, I've seen Trevor and he is something to lay eyes on. I've heard Evan is the most handsome."

"So?"

"So what if you take one look at him and your knees go weak, your heart goes pitterpat and you completely forget Trevor?" Amelia laid back on the bed. "What if he really is your Prince Charming?"

"Nonsense," Maddie said. "He would take one look at me and run screaming. I'm not exactly a Cinderella. Look at me, I'm twenty-five years old. My face is bruised and swollen. I'm wearing a dress I do chores in. I've lied and schemed and . . . kissed his brother. Why would Evan want me?"

Amelia sat up. "Well, now that you put it that way . . ."

"I need to go tell Papa."

"Wait. Let's see what I can do to fix you up."

"Why?"

"Mrs. Selis and Mrs. Lance are downstairs. If you don't

look better they're going to wonder why, and you need to talk to Papa before you talk to them. In fact, you need to talk to the Montgomerys before you talk to them, and you want to look your best when you do."

Maddie took a deep breath and blew it out. "Right."

Amelia pushed Maddie down and undid the pins in her hair. Then she picked up the brush and began to brush through her long locks.

"You know," Amelia said. "If Evan comes to call, Trevor will too. I mean, men don't just show up alone."

"So?"

"So, if you come down the stairs looking like a princess, we could have them at each other's throats fighting over you."

"Oh, Amelia, you have read far too many stories. It is more likely that they will both wish they had come to see Beth."

"What can it hurt? If you have to go down, you might as well go down gracefully."

"Well, you do have a point."

Amelia put down the brush, jumped off the bed and went to the armoire. "I have a lovely day dress that should fit you. I was saving it for the harvest dance, but what the heck." She pulled out a green gown. It was cut simply with a square bodice and short capped sleeves.

"Oh, Amelia, it's lovely."

"Of course it is. The way I see it, if you have to make a scene, you might as well make it looking as grand as possible."

Chapter Twelve

Trevor sat back and watched his brother charm his way into an extra piece of pie. The waitress at the hotel was all a flutter.

"Would you like another piece too?" she asked, not taking her eyes off Evan.

"No, thanks," Trevor said. Madeline's pie was so much better than what they offered at the hotel, he hadn't been able to finish the first. "Coffee's just fine."

He held out his cup and she refilled it. Trevor watched as she poured another cup for Evan. He smiled at her, and the little waitress went weak at the knees. Trevor's mood turned black. It had occurred to him that it might be possible that Madeline had loved Evan enough to wait eight years for him. Trevor wasn't sure he wanted to be around to see Maddie go weak in the knees.

"I should be getting back to the homestead," Trevor said. He twirled his hat on his knee. "The critters need to be fed and such."

"Oh, no, you don't," Evan said. "You're not going anywhere until we go see this gal."

"You're going to see her tonight?"

"I'm curious. Can't wait to see how good my taste was

when I was young." He grinned and took a bit of pie. "I bet she's stunning."

"She's something. She's been staying at the homestead, but now that you're home I doubt she'll come back out."

"You've been staying with her?"

"I've been out there," Trevor said and twisted his coffee cup around on its saucer. "I took ill and she stayed and nursed me."

Evan cocked his head and studied his brother. "Is something going on between you and my gal?"

Trevor was glad that he had a good poker face. He used it. He looked up slow and sober. "Madeline's not that kind of woman."

"Whoa," Evan said and held up his hand. "I wasn't accusing you of anything." He put his napkin on the table and pushed the plate away. "I was simply getting the lay of the land."

Trevor's thoughts turned to the kisses they had shared. If anything, his involvement with her was his own fault. "Madeline's waited eight years for you, Evan. The last thing she'd want to do is run off with me."

"Well," Evan said with a wide smile. "Come on then. Let's end the suspense and go see what happens when I meet my match."

Trevor's stomach soured. The thought of Maddie in Evan's arms was enough to leave him feeling like he'd been sucker-punched. Then he remembered how nervous she was whenever he talked about Evan. Hope blossomed in his heart. Maybe, just maybe, Maddie had changed her mind.

He glanced at his brother and noted how the ladies all smiled and flirted. Evan was younger. He had more charm and he was healthier. Worst of all, it was obvious that Evan had never killed anyone.

Maddie would have to be plain crazy to choose him over Evan. If he loved her, than he wouldn't let her. He stood and put his hat on. Then he left money for the dinner and a good tip.

Evan put his arm around Trevor's shoulder. "Thanks for dinner. I promise I'll pay you back as soon as I'm flush again."

Maddie held her head high as she descended the stairs. Thanks to Amelia, she looked better than she had looked in a long time. Maddie realized her sister was right. If you were going to meet your doom, you might as well do it looking like a princess.

She had been hiding upstairs for nearly two hours. Finally, Beth had run up and reported that once again like mother hens the ladies refused to leave until Maddie came down. So, she held her chin up and came downstairs.

"Maddie, dear, you look lovely," Mrs. Lance said.

"There, see? All it took was some good grooming," Mrs. Selis said. "I bet you feel much better now."

"Yes, in fact I do," Maddie said. "If you ladies will please excuse me. I need to find Papa."

"Is he back from his meeting?"

"I'll go see if Mrs. Poole knows," Maddie said.

"Well, my goodness girl," Mrs. Selis said. "It's not as if you are attending a funeral. Smile." Maddie bared her teeth. "That's much better. Now go on, scoot. Find your father." She took a sip of her tea. "Please let him know that we miss his company."

Maddie bit her tongue to keep from saying something rude, and walked down the hall to her father's office. She knew he was hiding in there and it was time she braved the lion's den.

Heck, if things didn't work out she could always tell the ladies that her father would love some female company. She smiled to herself as she knocked on the door. The threat of Mrs. Selis was something she could bargain.

"Come in."

Maddie took a deep breath and opened the door. Her father stood in the window looking out to the inky blackness of the evening. He puffed on his fat cigar and clasped his hands behind his back.

"Hello, Maddie. I wondered what was taking you so long." He turned and studied her. "You look lovely."

"Thank you," she said. Her heart pounded and she raised her chin. "Papa, we have to talk about this whole Montgomery affair."

"Let me guess—you don't love the lad."

The words dried up on Maddie's tongue. "How did you know?"

"Come on, girl. I'm not entirely without wits."

Maddie dug her fingers into the top of the wing-backed chair that faced her father's desk. "How long have you known?"

"Actually, I've always known."

"And yet you went along with it?"

"When I first declared that you must marry first, I thought I was being so clever. You were so lovely and so alone." He glanced at her. "It made my heart sad. I thought it would do you good to let the community know that you were looking for a suitor."

"You weren't counting on the Schyler brothers and their reward."

"No, I hadn't imagined that." He turned back to the window. "Still, I thought you could handle yourself and eventually some suitable man would show up at our door."

"What made you change your mind?"

"It was the day Smitherton shuffled onto the porch. Instead of turning him down cold, you looked at him with a thoughtful eye." He shuddered. "I knew then that you were desperate." He puffed on his stogie. "It seemed I'd opened a Pandora's box and I didn't know how to make it stop."

"Robert did."

"Yes," her father said to the window. "Robert found a

way." He shrugged. "When the ladies demanded that I rescue you from the suitors, I complied."

"Why didn't you tell me?"

"I was going to, but then the petition happened and the mayor made his declaration, and well . . ." He glanced over his shoulder at her. "I didn't think you would take it."

"I tried to refuse it," Maddie said and sat down on the chair she had been clutching moments before. "But the ladies had me packed and moved before I could. Then Robert asked me what it would possibly hurt if I did move in? After all, the Montgomerys had been gone so many years and that lovely home was going to ruin."

"I always knew Robert would be a good politician. He can talk a cow right out of her spots."

"What do we do now?" Maddie asked. Relieved that her father wasn't hurt by what had happened, she still was at a loss as to how to handle the situation.

"Deciding to come home was the best first step." He strode over and lifted Maddie's chin. His gaze went to the bruises on her cheek and he tisked his tongue. "I would have never let you stay if I had known it wasn't safe."

"Wait. If you knew it was a lie, why didn't you come and get me when Trevor came home?"

"I know you, Madeline. You're like your mother, very strong. So, I let Doc Emerson talk me into letting you stay and nurse him." He paused and studied her. "He didn't hurt you did he?"

"Trevor? No. Trevor is a kind, and caring man. In fact he saved my life this morning."

"I see."

Maddie stood at the tone of her father's voice. There were some things a daughter didn't want her father to see. "Everyone thinks Evan is going to come here and fall instantly in love with me."

"He'd be a fool if he didn't," her father said, and sat down behind his desk.

Her father's words were a gentle lashing on Maddie's heart. "I love you too, Papa."

"Even after I've put you in this predicament?"

She went over and put her arms around her father's neck. "Thank you for sharing the blame, but this is really my fault. I let the lie continue."

"What are you going to do now?"

"I don't know."

"Why don't we take it one moment at a time?" he asked, and patted her hands. "Whose to say this Evan won't fall in love with you."

Maddie gave a self-deprecating laugh. "So, the best thing in the world would be for Evan to fall instantly in love with me and ask me to marry him?"

"Is there anyone else?"

She pulled away. "No," she said carefully. Her thoughts turned to Trevor and the kiss they had shared this morning. Then she thought of how disappointed and horrified he would be now that he knew the truth. "There's no one else who has asked me to marry him."

"Then give the boy a chance," her Papa said. "He can't be too bad if Robert thought of him in the first place."

"Hmm."

"Unless you really do want to be a spinster," he said, his tone odd. "If that's the case you need to tell me here and now."

Maddie wrapped her arms around her waist and sighed. "Living alone for the past two years has taught me a lot," she said carefully. "I thought it would be nice to have no one to attend to but myself, but I was wrong. It's lonely, Papa. So very lonely. Then when Trevor came, it was . . . nice to have a man in the house."

"So, you aren't adverse to marrying."

"No, I'm not adverse," she said and turned to her father. "I didn't want to be like Beth and jump at the first man who asked me." She shook her head. "I still don't."

"Well, whoever asks you, he won't be the first," her Papa said gently. "There were the other suitors."

Maddie smiled at the memory and then laughed to see her father grinning too. "I certainly can hold my own, can't I?"

"Yes," he said, and put his arm around her. "I never have worried about you being pushed around."

"Except now my reputation is ruined."

"We'll cross that bridge as we come to it."

"Hmm." Maddie squeezed her hands together. Her thoughts went to Trevor. Once the truth came out he would never look at her again. How she would miss his wry smile and the sweet honest sound of his fiddle.

"I'm not certain I can stay in town if everyone knows," she said honestly. "I'm certain everyone will know—Mrs. Selis and Mrs. Lance are still in the parlor."

"Not to worry," Papa replied. "We'll go on holiday to Chicago for a while. Chicago is a big city. There is a good chance you will meet a fine young man there. If not, at the very least it will give this time to blow over."

"What are we going to do about the ladies?"

"Let them stew," her father said, and poured himself a whiskey. "I, for one, refuse to go out there."

"Papa!"

"That Mrs. Selis looks at me like a hunter sizing up a twelve-point buck. Forget it, I'm staying out of her sights."

Maddie laughed. Somehow just knowing that her father feared the ladies buoyed her confidence. No matter what happened next she could handle it.

Trevor walked with his brother to the Morgan house. His legs were wooden and he felt as if he was on his way to his own funeral. Evan on the other hand was light-hearted. He was still commenting on how the waitress had flirted with him.

"This is it," Trevor said, and stopped at the gate to the little picket fence that surrounded the large house.

"Nice place," Evan said. "I forget. What's her father do?"

"He owns the local mill," Trevor said, "and he raises the best horses in the county."

"Things just keep getting better and better," Evan said with a grin. He slapped Trevor on the back. "Come on, brother, let's go meet this paragon of virtue."

Trevor gritted his teeth and followed his brother through the fence and up onto the porch.

"You knock," Evan said. "I'll hang back and then you can introduce me, or should I say reintroduce me." Evan grinned and two dimples popped out. It was a smile that had girls swooning and Trevor knew it. Right now he hated it.

"Fine." He knocked and the housekeeper opened the door. "Good evening," Trevor said, and took his hat off. He twisted it in his hand. "Is Miss Madeline home?"

"Certainly, won't you come in?" The housekeeper opened the door wide and waited for them to come in.

Trevor stepped inside. Evan followed behind him. It was the first time Trevor had ever been inside the Morgan home. It was large and stately. There was a foyer with stairs running up to the right. To the left was a wide door that probably opened to the parlor. Down the hall was a closet that opened under the stairs and two more doors.

The foyer was paneled in wood with homey rugs on the floor and a portrait of a woman. Trevor looked at it closely. The woman resembled Madeline and Beth. She appeared to be about Beth's age and he could only assume it was a picture of their mother.

"Please come inside," the housekeeper said when she reappeared. "Madeline and her family are in the parlor visiting with Mrs. Selis and Mrs. Lance."

Mrs. Selis and Mrs. Lance. Trevor had to work to hide

his disgust. The two busybodies had cornered him on the street and questioned him intently about Maddie, and whether he knew anything at all about when Evan was coming home. At the time he'd been a bit bemused and completely clueless.

Now he knew exactly why the ladies had come calling. They wanted to see firsthand Evan's and Maddie's happy reunion. He'd be darned if he was the one to make it happen.

Trevor followed the housekeeper into the parlor. Maddie rose when they entered and Trevor's jaw dropped. She was stunning in a green day gown he'd never seen her wear. Her hair was done up in a fancy way and though he could still see the bruise on her face, she had covered it well with powder.

"Please come in, we were just talking about the—"

She stopped short when Evan stepped into the room. Suddenly, she stumbled, her words coming to a complete halt as her gaze feasted on his brother.

Trevor swallowed his anger and grief. "Madeline."

Beth jumped to her feet. "Evan and Trevor Morgan. Please come in. Evan, I'm Maddie's sister Beth. I was ten when you and Maddie were courting so you probably don't remember me."

"How could I forget someone as lovely as you?" Evan said, turning on the charm. He took Beth's hand and kissed it.

"Goodness," Beth said flustered. "Do you know my sister, Amelia?" She waved toward a woman who looked to be about twenty. Trevor took in the dark auburn hair and splash of freckles covered by a pair of horn-rimmed glasses.

Amelia stood up. Her gaze darted from Evan to Maddie and back as if she was waiting for the world to end.

"Hello, Amelia," Evan said. Then he turned to Maddie.

He reached out and brushed the back of his hand along his cheek. "Hello, Madeline."

"Hello," she barely got out. Trevor gripped his hat hard. Maddie looked as stunned as she did when Angel cuffed her.

"You turned out quite beautiful," Evan said.

Maddie blushed that lovely pink. It rushed up and over her cheeks and Trevor knew he would never be the same.

"Ladies," Evan said when he turned to the other women on the settee. "We're sorry to come barging in on your visit, but it has been such a long time since I've been in town and since I've been to the Morgan household. I'd forgotten how lovely the women are."

Trevor wanted to kill someone when he saw the look his brother sent Maddie.

"Please, don't worry about us," Mrs. Selis said. "We can visit another time. Mrs. Lance."

"Oh, yes, of course, we should leave you young people to visit." The second woman rose. She giggled as she passed by. "We'll be seeing you again soon," Mrs. Lance said. "Good night ladies."

"Good night," Beth and Amelia said in unison.

Trevor noted how quiet Maddie was. It seemed she couldn't take her eyes off Evan. Trevor felt sullen. It was all he could do not to plop his hat on his head and follow the old biddies out the door.

"Please sit down, gentlemen," Beth said.

"Would you like some tea?" Amelia asked.

"I was wondering if Madeline would come out walking with me?" Evan said. Trevor noted with disgust how his brother's gaze took in the treasure he'd left behind.

Maddie glanced at Trevor and his heart broke into a million pieces. Her gaze held a question. He nodded. "I told him and he wanted to see you right away."

He wanted to stop her and tell her that Evan didn't even remember her. He wanted to say that Evan wasn't worthy of her, but he kept his mouth shut. Evan was the man she waited for, not Trevor. He had to give her time.

Amelia disappeared through a doorway and reappeared with a coat in her hands. "It's chilly out there. You'd better bundle up."

Trevor clutched his hat as he watched Maddie put on the sturdy wool coat and matching gloves. "Would you like to come with us?" she asked him.

The last thing he wanted to do was witness their joyful reunion. "No, thanks, I need to get back to the homestead." He jammed his hat on his head and opened the door. "Someone has to feed the animals."

"Keep a light on for me," Evan said and grinned. "I think I can remember the way."

Disgruntled, Trevor gave his brother a short nod and disappeared into the cool quiet of the night air. The crunch of his boots on the stone walkway wasn't the only sound he heard. There was also the tearing of his heart.

Chapter Thirteen

Evan Morgan held out his arm and smiled at Maddie. She was bemused. Trevor was angry but had not confronted her, and Evan smiled indulgently at her. His grin was so charming. His manner so refined. It was the oddest thing. He acted as if they had courted, as if the lie was the truth. She had no clue how to handle the situation so she placed her hand on the crook of his arm and followed him out into the cool night air.

Silence wrapped around them. She was filled with trepidation and wondered if it would be better for her to simply blurt out the truth or wait for him to confront her.

She decided that she'd waited this long, a little longer wouldn't hurt. She bit her bottom lip and simply walked beside him.

He opened the little gate and ushered her through. Maddie glanced down the street, but Trevor was already gone. What she did notice was the tiny movements of curtains in the houses nearby.

"I think you should know that we're being watched from every window in town," she warned him.

"Now why would they do that?"

"Curious, I guess."

"Because I've been away for so long or because you've waited for me for so long?"

Maddie looked at him. His expression was unreadable in the cool night air. "I'm sorry. What I did was completely wrong."

"What are you sorry for? Waiting eight years for my return or that you've pretended to be so smitten that no other man will do?" He patted her hand and grinned at her. "Or are you sorry that the whole town thinks we're in love and is right now planning our wedding."

"All of it, I guess," she said and blew out a deep breath. "Some story, huh?"

"It's a classic."

"So, why did you come to my house? Why not simply denounce me right off?"

He grinned. "To bother my brother."

"Trevor?"

"Yeah, he's angry about the way I treated you."

"But you didn't."

"Well, now, I wasn't sure. You see I couldn't remember ever asking someone to marry me, but . . ." He shrugged. "I might have in a drunken stupor. Then I saw you and I knew. You are obviously not the kind of woman a man proposes to in a drunken stupor."

"If I were?"

"If you were, then I was going to come here tonight and let you down easy."

"So you're off the hook. I'm the one who made the mess, not you."

"Yeah," he said and glanced around. "You know, I hate to say this but what I do remember of your family, this seems more like the kind of thing your brother would do."

Maddie sent him a chagrined look. "It was Robert's idea."

He laughed. It was a clear sound that bounced off the

trees and echoed down the street. "How is old Rob, by the way?"

"He's in Wyoming. I'll send him your hello."

"You do that." He reached up and gently touched the bruise under her eye. "I owe you for this. If you want, I can spend the night in the saloon and tell everyone that you are the one who broke off the engagement."

"Please, you don't have to do anything that would ruin your reputation in town."

"I don't care about this town. Heck, I only stopped by to see if the old place was still there."

"It's still there and I fixed it up a little."

"Yeah, Trevor told me. He said you planted mums on Ma's grave. I think she'd like that."

Maddie sighed. "You know, you're a nice man, Evan Montgomery. I'm sorry for involving you in this whole thing."

He laughed even harder. "Honey, if you think I'm a nice man then you really don't know me at all." He took her hand and started back toward her house.

"So what are we going to do now, Madeline Morgan?"

She glanced at his handsome profile. "I suppose you can go on living your life. Me, I've got to finally tell the truth and face the consequences."

"If you ever need anyone to stand up for you, you holler. Like I said, I owe you and I might be an ornery critter, but I pay my debts."

"Thank you, Evan."

He opened the tiny picket gate that led to her front porch. Then he tugged on his hat and grinned. "How about a kiss for old time sake?"

She shook her head and couldn't help the smile that crept over her face. "You are a rascal and much kinder than I deserve."

"I beg to differ with you," he said, his expression sober.

"I beg to differ." He leaned down and brushed a kiss against her unbruised cheek. "Take care, Maddie Morgan."

"Good bye, Evan."

He stepped away and she watched him walk down the street toward the stables. She blew out a breath. It was over. Now she had to go inside and figure out how she was going to tell the rest of the town. She headed up the porch stairs.

"When's the wedding?" came a voice from beside the house.

Startled, Maddie looked to see Trevor leaning against the house, his hands in his pockets. He looked angrier than a wet hen.

"I beg your pardon?"

He stepped up onto the porch. "You and Evan. I saw him kiss you. So, when's the wedding?"

"For your information there isn't going to be a wedding," Maddie said. She tried to brush past him, but he grabbed her by the wrist and turned her toward him.

"So, you're simply in the habit of kissing men?"

She slapped him for that. The action surprised the both of them. Her eyes widened and her pulse raced. "I'm sorry," she said. The heat of embarrassment followed closely behind the deep insult that caused her to act before she thought.

"I suppose I deserved that," he conceded and rubbed the red mark on his cheek. "Let me try that again. Welcome to the family, Maddie. I hope you are both happy." He sneered the last part, insulting her yet again.

"What is the matter with you?" His words had slashed through her heart, hurting her in ways she didn't know she could be hurt. "You make it sound as if I'm not good enough to marry someone like your brother. I realize I'm no spring chicken, but—"

He let out a roar of laughter. She fisted her hands and placed them on her hips as her anger grew. "Stop laughing at me."

He sobered. "Honey, your age has nothing to do with it."

"Then what is it? You've been hounding me from the moment we met. What do you want from me, Trevor Montgomery?"

"I want you to be happy. You once said that you lived up to no one's expectations but your own."

"So?"

"So whose expectations are you living up to if you go through with this marriage? The town's? Mrs. Selis'? Evan's?"

"You have a lot of room to talk," she snapped. "I don't see you putting in any of those improvements to the farm you talked about."

"It's Evan's now."

"Why? Because you think he proposed to me? Please, that's just a good excuse for you to run away from your childhood dreams."

"I'm not running."

"No? Henry said he saw you talking to Albert Henson about Wyoming. Why would you do that?"

"There's opportunity there."

"There's opportunity here too," she said. "Not that you've stuck around long enough to see it."

"What do you want me to do? Take the farm from Evan?"

"Did Evan tell you he wanted the farm?"

"Not exactly."

"So you're assuming that he wants you to shove off and leave it to him."

"Two's company, three's a crowd."

She shook her head. "I'm going inside."

"Wait."

She turned on her heel and looked at him. She could have told him then that he didn't need to worry. She wasn't going to marry his brother. In fact, she highly doubted she would ever marry anyone once the truth came out. But he was so insulting she decided to let him stew. He'd hear about it from Evan when he got home.

"I'll stay if you want me to," he finally said.

"This isn't about what I want, Trevor." Sadness filled her. What she wanted would never happen. Not now, not when the truth came out. She realized then that she really was a fallen woman. "This is about what you want. If you really want to go to Wyoming, then go. There's no one here that's going to stop you."

"Madeline."

"Yes, Trevor?"

"Promise me something."

"What?"

"Promise me that whatever you do, you'll be happy."

"I can't promise that. But what I can promise you is that I will make the right decision. That has to be enough for both of us. Good night, Trevor."

"Good night, Maddie."

She opened her front door and closed it sharply. Then she leaned against it. What a mess she made of everything. She heard Trevor take the two steps off the porch, his boots crunching on the front path as he left. Her heart left with him. She blew out a breath and knew it was time to face the music. Her family waited in the parlor to find out what happened.

"What are you doing?" Trevor asked Evan. He walked into the house to find his brother going through the books on the shelves.

"I left some cash stashed here," Evan said, and pulled out a book. He reached behind it and brought out a small box. "That's why I came home actually."

"Wait. I thought you came back to stay?"

"I never said anything about staying."

Trevor's thoughts went to Maddie. She hadn't mentioned

anything about leaving. He narrowed his eyes. "But I thought you came back to work the farm?"

"What, me work?" Evan grinned. "Please, Trevor, when have I ever been interested in the old homestead?"

"You never intended to stay?"

"Nope. The place is all yours, big brother. Work it with my blessing."

"What are you going to do?"

"I have a hot prospect in Kansas City. Heard there's a saloon for sale. I thought I'd give that a whirl."

"What about Madeline?"

"What about her?" Evan said with a shrug, and opened the box. He pulled out a wad of bills and shoved them in his pockets.

"Is she okay with your going to Kansas City?"

"I don't know, I didn't ask her."

"You didn't ask her?"

"I don't see how it's any of her business."

Anger crept down Trevor's back. It was bad enough that Evan was engaged to Madeline. Trevor couldn't stand to see her mistreated. "She's going to be your wife, man. I think that makes it her business."

Evan put the book back on the shelf. "I'm not marrying Madeline," he said. He ignored Trevor and went into the kitchen and poured himself a cup of coffee.

"What do you mean, you're not going to marry Madeline?" Trevor asked. Shock displaced the anger, and to his shame Trevor also felt hope.

"I mean, I'm not marrying her," Evan said, and sat down at the table. He threw his long legs out in front of him and crossed his ankles.

"But—"

"Look, brother, the fact is I never asked Maddie to marry me."

"You never asked her to marry you?"

"Nope. It was a story her brother Robert made up."

"But you acted as though—"

"Well, you never can tell. Eight years is a long time." Evan shrugged and blew across his coffee cup. "That is until I saw her." He glanced up. "Seems to me that Madeline Morgan's not the kind of woman you'd forget."

Trevor grabbed the back of the chair and leaned on it. "She's not your fiancée?"

"Nope."

"She never was your fiancée?"

"Nope." He took a sip of his coffee. "Still, it looks like she kept the place up real nice." He raised an eyebrow at his brother. "I'd hate to see her shunned for it."

"She never was your fiancée."

"I already said she wasn't."

"And she didn't try to get you to marry her?"

"Nope, in fact, she apologized real nice for the trouble she caused. Too bad I didn't meet her sooner."

"What do you mean by that?"

"What I mean is, any man in his right mind wanting to settle down would take one look at her and drop down on his knee."

"But you didn't."

"I said a man wantin' to settle down. Me, I'm on my way out of town. I kind of like driftin'. Do you know what I mean?"

"So, you're on your way out the door."

Evan grinned. "I figure I have the money I came for. You have the farm. It all worked out for the best." He finished his coffee. "Look, I don't know what your plans are. But you can sell the place if you don't want it. I don't need the cash."

"What about Ma's grave?"

"Put a little fence around it. I'm sure it'll be fine." He stood. "As for me, I've got to leave in the morning if I hope to make Kansas City by the end of the week." He stretched. "Well, I'm off to bed. It was great seeing you again. Sorry about Angel. I don't think that's going to happen again."

"It better not," Trevor said sternly. "I'm done with killing men."

"So, you're going to give farming a try?"

"Yeah," Trevor said, and gave his brother a quick hug. "Keep your nose clean. Okay?"

"Okay."

Something close to joy filled Trevor. Madeline was not going to marry Evan. That meant he had a chance, but first he had some things to do.

The meeting of the Boltonville Ladies Brigade started promptly at 2 P.M. The whole town was a twitter about Evan Montgomery's return. Everyone she passed on the streets smiled and nodded or tipped their hats. Maddie knew that wouldn't last. Not once they knew the truth.

Maddie glanced in the windows of the meeting hall and blew out a breath. It was time to face the consequences of her actions. She had dressed in a proper suit; worsted wool, navy blue, it buttoned up the front. Short gloves buttoned at her wrists. Even her hat matched, with a smart plume flying like a flag of truth.

"Come on," Maddie said to her sisters and Mrs. Poole. The entire female population of the Morgan clan had banded together to show Maddie support. It was nice to know that she wasn't going to go down alone.

She flung the meeting hall doors open and marched up the center aisle. All sound in the hall stopped. Not a single giggle was heard.

"Ah, Maddie," Mrs. Selis said. "Come on up, we were just discussing you." The conversation in the room grew around her.

Maddie's heart raced at the sound of whispers but she stayed the course. "Mrs. Selis," she said as she approached the dais. "Ladies of the Boltonville Brigade." She stepped up to the podium. "If I might take a moment of your meeting time, there is something I must say."

"Certainly, dear," Mrs. Selis said. She slammed the gavel on the podium. "Ladies, please. Madeline Morgan wishes to address the assembly."

"Thank you." Maddie waited for Mrs. Selis to sit down before she faced the women of Boltonville. "Good afternoon, ladies." She paused while they greeted her en masse. "I have come today with my sisters to straighten out an unfortunate misunderstanding. A misunderstanding that I've allowed to go on far too long."

A wave of whispers started at her words. She raised her hand to halt it. "Please." Silence filled the hall. "Thank you. Let me first begin by thanking each and every one of you for your support over the last two years. I know it was meant out of love and kindness of your hearts." She paused while they nodded and smiled. "My mother would be proud of the good care and direction you have provided." The crowd nodded and whispered their pride at her acknowledgement. Her heart picked up speed and she wrapped her fingers around the podium for support, then lifted her chin. "I am here today to tell you all that I have deceived you."

"What?!" The crowd grew restless and concerned.

"My brother Robert made up the story of my engagement." She swallowed at the shock and disbelief on their faces. "I allowed the rumor to spread and take over. I had no idea of the extent of your kindness." She glanced at the wedding gown her sister Amelia carried and motioned for Amelia to put the gown on a nearby table. "It was Robert's thought that Evan was dead and I could spend the rest of my life as a war widow."

"But Evan isn't dead," someone said. "He's here. You can marry him."

"I was never in love with Evan Montgomery." She saw a motion in the rear of the room and noted that the mayor had come into the back of the room. "I didn't deserve the deed to their homestead. I want you to know that I gave it back to Trevor. Now, I'm here to give you back the beautiful dress that you made and to tell you that I'm very sorry."

Mrs. Selis stepped over to the podium. "I'm certain Maddie misspoke. If this is your idea of a practical joke, well, it's simply not funny."

Maddie swallowed hard. "It's not a joke. It's all true."

"But you spent weeks out on that farm alone with Trevor Morgan."

"Trevor was sick and Doc Emerson said he needed me to nurse him. I stayed because it was the least I could do for Trevor. After all, I had been living in his house under false pretenses."

The crowd no longer whispered its speculation and shock. Maddie heard everyone speak at once.

"Disgrace!"

"Her poor dead mother!"

"I would never have believed it!"

Maddie took the gavel from Mrs. Selis' shocked hand and pounded it on the podium. "Ladies, please."

Someone shouted out. "That doesn't mean you can't marry Evan anyway." The crowd grew silent and nodded in agreement. Maddie shook her head.

"You don't understand. I don't love him." She tried to hold her voice together. Her gaze went straight to old Mrs. Addlestone. "Are you okay, Mrs. Addlestone?"

"Certainly," she said and frowned. "You're the one who is nuts. Did you take a good look at the boy?" She shook her head. "I ain't seen nothing that nice to look at in over fifty years."

Maddie ignored the old woman's grumbling. "Please listen to me. I was never in love with Evan Montgomery." She paused to let that sink in. "We never courted. There was no secret engagement."

"But we heard . . ." Mrs. Selis said.

"The mayor said . . ." Mrs. Lance added.

"All rumors that got out of hand," Maddie said firmly. "I went along with it because I knew it made you all so happy." She glanced at the wedding gown. "It gave you something positive in this dark time when our men are still straggling home from a war long over.

"It gave you hope and it allowed me to live free, but then when Evan came home, I simply couldn't continue to live the lie."

"So, there's not going to be a wedding?" someone from the audience called out.

"No," Maddie said. "There is not going to be a wedding."

"No dance? No pot luck?"

It seemed they couldn't comprehend what she was trying to tell them. She looked at the crowd of disappointed faces. "Okay, sure, why not have a dance and a pot luck?" Maddie suggested. "We could celebrate the work you all have done for the ladies of this community. In fact, we could make it a reverse dance and let the gals ask the men. What do you think about that?"

"I can't believe you lied to us," Mrs. Selis said as she snapped out of her shock.

"We can even have a parade and Blanche Selis can be the grand marshal," Maddie said, and put the gavel into the older woman's hand before she could think. "After all, she is the very nature of womankind today; strong, and independent yet with a soft side. What do you think ladies? Shall we have a dance and a parade?" The crowd cheered. Maddie smiled. She pushed Mrs. Selis toward the podium. "Shall we name Blanche the grand marshal?"

More cheers erupted.

Mrs. Selis recovered from her surprise with aplomb. A gleam of righteousness sparkled in her eye as she banged the gavel down.

Maddie eased down the side aisle. She could hear Mrs.

Selis as she began to organize the parade. She barked out orders like a sergeant.

Maddie's sisters and Mrs. Poole left with Maddie. Each had a smile on her face. They stepped outside and Maddie felt a great weight lift off her shoulders.

"You handled that very well," Amelia said with a wry smile. "A parade?"

"I had to do something, Mrs. Selis was going to explode. Besides, by the time they're done with the planning they will have forgotten all about me."

"Too bad about the dress," Beth said with a heavy sigh. "It sure was pretty."

"A pretty dress does not make a marriage," Maddie said with a shake of her head. "Just a lot of hard work, so there has to be love to motivate you to get through the hard work."

"Maddie?"

"Yes, Beth?"

"Do you think you'll ever fall in love?"

Maddie fought the heavy sigh that threatened to come out. "Just being in love by yourself isn't enough. Both people have to be in love or it's simply not worth it.

Now, let's go home and make some lemonade."

Chapter Fourteen

That afternoon Maddie sat in her father's den. She had darning in her lap, but instead of working she found herself staring out the window. The day itself had become quite bright and almost warm. She knew it was fall's last hurrah before the cold and dark of winter set in. But even the lovely sunshine couldn't fill the emptiness in her heart.

By now the whole town knew that she had deceived them all. Everyone was aware that she had spent three weeks alone with Trevor. She bit her bottom lip and worried that her ruined reputation would affect her sisters. She hoped not.

"Maddie, there you are." Amelia stuck her head inside the room. "I've been looking all over for you."

"I was working on the darning," Maddie said then shook her head. "Actually, I was gathering a little wool. What did you need?"

"You have to come out to the parlor. You have a visitor."

"A visitor?"

"More than one."

Maddie swallowed. Who could possibly want to visit with her now unless it was Mrs. Selis and Mrs. Lance come to berate her? "Tell them I'm indisposed."

"I could," Amelia said frankly and stepped into the room. "But you're going to have to face the world some time and they're here now, waiting for you."

Maddie took a deep breath and blew it out slow. Of course they were. "All right, I'll see them." She stood up and put the sock and ball back into the basket that held the mending.

"You might want to check your hair," Amelia said with a twinkle in her eye.

Maddie frowned and glanced in the mirror over the hearth. "I look fine."

"Good, now come on." Amelia took Maddie's hand and pulled her down the hall.

Maddie prepared herself for the onslaught to come. She decided that the best way to handle a lecture was to nod and express her thankfulness that the ladies cared so much, regardless of the fact that they had a heavy hand in her predicament.

She rounded the corner and came to a complete stop. There on the couch sat Stuart Bixley clutching a rather wilted group of mums. Beside him sat Mr. Smitherton. The old man had nodded off, his chin resting on his thin chest.

"Mmmadeline," Stuart said and stood up. The motion jerked the old man awake. "Thhese are for you." He held out the flowers.

Mr. Smitherton smacked Stuart with his cane and stood up. "Get out of my way, boy. I was here first. Rude to keep a man waiting this long."

Maddie glanced at Amelia whose smile was playful. "I'm sorry," Madeline said. "I don't understand."

"We heard you weren't engaged to that Montgomery boy," Mr. Smitherton said.

"Wooould you like to go out for a walk with me, Mmmaddie?"

"But there's no reward for marrying me."

"We know that," Smitherton said. "Now that you're a

fallen woman an all, we thought you might be in need of, well, marrying."

"What?!"

"Wwwe don't care that yyyou're fallen," Stuart said. "It kinda makes yyyou more interestin'."

"I'm sorry, I'm not certain I understand. You are both here to court me?"

"Yep!"

The idea was so far from her thoughts that she had to sit down. The men waited until she took the chair across from them, then Stuart handed her the sweat-covered wilted flowers and sat down. Maddie stared at the flowers in her hand. After two years and so much deception she was right back where she started.

"Mmmaddie?"

"Well, girl, whatcha got to say for yourself?" Mr. Smitherton said, and banged his cane on the floor to get her attention.

Maddie had to laugh, the whole thing was so ridiculous. She took one look at the hope in Stuart's eyes and her heart had pity on him. "Well," she said, trying to feel her way out of this predicament. "I never expected anyone to come calling and so soon after the truth had come out."

"So, are you interested or not?" the old man demanded.

"Well, I—"

"Excuse me, Madeline, but you have a couple of visitors at the door," Mrs. Poole said, and with a wave of her hand two more men stepped into the parlor.

Maddie stood up. "Bud Brown, Sam Waterstein, what brings you gentlemen—" She noticed that they carried flowers in their hands and panic shot through her. "Oh, dear."

"Maddie, I thought maybe since you were free an' all, you'd like to step out with me," Sam said, his gray eyes twinkling.

"Hey, I got to the door first," Bud declared. "Here Maddie, these are for you." He stuck out the handful of flowers, but Sam pushed them aside.

"The only reason you got here first is because you jumped the fence," Sam said and turned to Maddie. "These are real hothouse flowers, not something I picked out of Maybelle Green's garden."

"I did not pick these, I paid for these." The two men were suddenly toe to toe.

"Gentlemen!" Maddie said as sternly as she could. "Sit down and we'll discuss this like grownups." She pointed to the chairs on the opposite ends of the room. The two new suitors slunk to the chairs.

"We gggot here first," Stuart complained.

"Maddie."

"What!" She turned to where Amelia stood in the doorway. Three more men stood behind her, hats and flowers in hand. "Oh my," she said resignedly. "Come on in, the more the merrier." The men grinned and made their way around Amelia, each handing Maddie their flowers. The pile grew in her arms and she glanced at her sister for help.

"I'll go get Papa," Amelia said, and disappeared down the hall.

Maddie thanked the Lord that her sister had a good head on her shoulders. "If you gentlemen will excuse me a moment," Maddie said as calmly as she could. "I need to put these flowers in water."

They all stood when she moved and waited as she left the room. There was a knock on the front door as Maddie entered the foyer. Mrs. Poole answered it as serenely as possible. Four more men stood on the porch in their best courtin' clothes. They grinned at Maddie as they came in, handed her flowers, and stepped into the parlor.

Maddie's arms were loaded with sweet blooms. There was another knock at the door which spurred her into action. Maddie sailed down the hall and into the kitchen. She needed a moment alone to collect her thoughts and, for goodness sakes, get the flowers into water.

Trevor found her late that evening, sitting on the stump in a small clearing in the middle of the wood. She hugged her shawl around her shoulders and stared up at the stars that twinkled in the ink-black sky.

She looked so lovely it hurt. The moonlight bounced off her fair skin and, for the first time, Trevor felt a little nervous. There was a right way to do this and a wrong way to do this. He hoped his way was right.

"Hello."

She kept her gaze up on the stars. "They really do make you feel small."

He looked up a second then back down at her. "Kind of chilly to be sitting out here alone." He took a deep breath and let it out slow, hoping to calm the butterflies in his stomach. "Mind if I join you?"

She let out a short self-deprecating laugh. "Sure, why not?"

He managed to take up the rest of the space on the stump without touching her. The problem was he wanted to touch her. He wanted to hold her and dance with her and kiss her senseless. Heck, if he was being honest with himself, he wanted to pick her up, throw her over his shoulder and take her home. Then he would see that she never left again. That's what he'd do if it was up to him. It wasn't.

"I got the note you sent around this afternoon," he said, and wiped his hands down his thighs. He kept his gaze on the sky. "Nice penmanship."

She blew out a breath. "I suppose the written apology was the coward's way out." She looked at him. "You deserve better than that. I'm sorry about the whole thing. I'll understand if you want some sort of restitution. Papa'll pay you whatever you think is fair."

"So, it really is true. You were never engaged to my brother."

"Robert made the whole thing up and I never refuted it. That was wrong. I know that now." She shook her head and clutched her hands together. "I should have told you the moment you arrived home. I meant to, but somehow it all kept on going. I guess I secretly wanted to belong in your house. I think I fell in love with the place and your mother's things."

"That's evident in the way you cared for everything, and since I hadn't said so before, let me say so now. Thank you."

"For what?"

"For taking care of the homestead, for making everything right, and most of all for caring for me while I was ill."

She blinked. "I don't understand. You aren't angry? I mean, I thought . . . well, shoot, of course you aren't angry. You got exactly what you wanted, me out of your house and away from your brother." She stood up. "I have to go."

"Wait!" He snagged her elbow and stood up. She turned and looked at him, her expression unreadable. She looked so sad and lost. He wanted to hold her and keep on holding her forever. "Are you okay?"

She sent him a small smile. "I'm fine. You have been nothing but kind." She shrugged away from him. "Good night, Trevor." She took four steps away while he tried to figure out what to say next, what to do. He shoved his hands in his pockets.

"I heard tell you had a few visitors this afternoon."

She shook her head. "I don't think I'll ever understand the way men think."

"Heard you turned them all away. Why? Don't you want to get married?"

"Some day," she replied, and hugged her shawl around her. "If there's love involved."

He touched her then, running his hand along her shoulder

and down her arm. "I heard a couple of fellows declared that they loved you just this afternoon."

She looked at him, her eyes dark and mysterious. "But I don't love them."

His heart tripped at her words. Hope blossomed deep inside him. "Is there someone you love?"

"Yes." She looked away.

He reached over and gently drew her gaze back to his. "Does this person love you back?"

"I don't know," she whispered.

"Was he one of the suitors?"

"No."

"Do you want him to be?"

"Yes," she replied her voice breathless. "But he won't be."

"Why not?" Trevor let go of her. If he touched her again he would kiss her and that was not the answer. At least not yet.

"The man I love does not deserve a woman who would lie and cheat." Her gaze returned to his. "No one that wonderful should settle for anything less than the best."

He didn't know what to say to that. In his eyes she was the best, but it was clear she didn't think so. He opened his mouth to tell her she was, to tell her that that was why so many men had come to her house, but he knew that she would not believe him. Not now anyway.

"So that's it? You're simply going to live the rest of your life in your father's house?"

"Good night, Trevor." She moved away, refusing to answer his question. It came to him in a blinding instant. He knew what he had to do. He had to show her exactly how much he loved her.

"Good night Maddie." The first thing he had to do was to go see Mrs. Selis and Mrs. Lance. In times like these a man needed all the help he could get.

* * *

Maddie stood in the backyard, hanging out the wash. She pushed a stray hair out of her face with the back of her hand and lifted a cold dripping shirt to the line. She pinned it with the wooden clothes pins that were clipped to the pocket of her work apron. She looked at her father's shirt and thought about washing Trevor's shirts. Two years ago, she had never imagined that she would daydream about someone's laundry, but now she knew that it felt good to express your love for someone by caring for them.

She blew out a breath and reached for another shirt. Her hands were red and raw from the wash, but not as raw as her heart.

She had turned away five more suitors this morning already. Even though she was dressed like a washerwoman, they didn't seem to care. It would be funny actually if it weren't happening to her. She appreciated the irony of ending up back where she started. Facing the countless men, young and old who wanted a piece of her heart.

This time it was no longer hers to give.

"Maddie, Maddie, come quick!" Beth scurried around the corner of the house. "The whole town is up in arms."

"What?" Maddie dropped the shirt back into the basket.

"You have to come. The men, they're fighting over you."

"Over me?" Maddie's heart raced as Beth took her hand and drew her around the house. As they got to the front porch, Amelia raced out.

"Maddie, it's just awful. I told Papa. He'll be right out."

"What's going on?"

Henry met them at the gate. "It's the men," he said breathlessly. "There's this huge fight. The sheriff has called in reinforcements."

Maddie raced down the street to the town square. People streamed out of their homes. The atmosphere was thick with tension. As they got closer, Maddie noticed a growing crowd. She elbowed her way through to find two men rising up from the ground while three more pummeled a man in the middle.

"Stop this!" she shouted. "Stop this at once."

"Don't worry yourself over this," Sam Waterstein said as he wiped the blood from the corner of his mouth. "This is between us and Montgomery."

"Montgomery?" Two of the three men hit the dirt and Trevor was left to duck the advances of the third.

"He ain't got no right saying that none of us can court you," Sam said and spit to the side. "No right at all."

"He said you can't court me?"

"Yep," Sam said. "An' he's willing to back it up with his fists." He nodded toward the fighters. Trevor landed a blow on the chin of the last man standing and he went down like a load of bricks.

"Stop this!" Maddie said. She fought her way through just as another man got up off the ground, dusted himself off and raised his fists as if to tell Trevor to try again. "Stop this at once!"

"Do what the little lady says," Sheriff Pickens said sternly, "or you'll all be tossed in jail for the night."

The men put down their fists but circled each other warily. Maddie could not believe it. "Trevor Montgomery, just what do you think you're doing?"

He eyed her then, wiped the blood off his rapidly swelling bottom lip and grinned. "Hello, Maddie."

"I want to know what you thought you were doing!" she demanded and put her hands on her hips. Horrified at the knot swelling on his chin, she clung to her anger to keep from embarrassing herself in front of the whole town.

"Why, I'm informing these gentlemen that you aren't up for courtship right now."

"Who gave you the right to do that?"

"Why, just last night you told me that you wanted to marry for love, didn't you?"

Maddie felt the flush of a blush rush over her face. She

glanced at the crowd that now consisted of every man, woman and child in Boltonville.

"Didn't you, Maddie?"

"I did."

"Then you told me that there was someone you loved already. Didn't you?"

She swallowed and swore that even the nearby field mice paused to hear her answer. "I did," she squeaked out.

His beautiful gaze darkened and he stepped closer. "Now, inform these gentlemen that you don't love them."

She was caught in the heat of his gaze. Her mind went blank and her mouth went dry as her heart sped up. He looked so handsome even with the growing knot on his chin. She wanted so badly to touch him.

"Maddie," he said. "Tell them that you aren't in love with any of them."

She glanced around. "I'm sorry," she said to the suitors. "Trevor is right. I'm not in love with any of you."

"Now, tell them who you are in love with, Maddie."

She glanced at him, as a prick of horror stabbed her.

"Tell them."

"I—"

"If a person is in love, than they shouldn't be ashamed of shouting it to the highest mountain top. Isn't that right, Mr. Morgan?"

"That's right."

Maddie glanced over her shoulder to see her father standing there, his expression oddly persuasive. "Tell him, Maddie."

Horrified, she glanced around at the expectant faces of the entire town. "I—I can't."

She glanced at Trevor. "I can't."

"Why not?" he asked. "These men all declared their love for you in front of the whole town. Are you saying that our brave and generous Maddie doesn't have the guts to do the same?"

"I—"

"Well, of course she doesn't." Ms. Selis stepped in. "No woman in her right mind is going to declare her love dressed like a washerwoman." There was a murmur of agreement from the ladies in the crowd. "Come on Maddie, let's get you changed."

Mrs. Lance took Maddie's arm and led her away.

"We'll settle this in fifteen minutes," Mrs. Selis said. "And might I suggest that you gentlemen get cleaned up as well? No woman wants to see her man looking like he's been in a bar brawl."

The crowd noise murmured louder and Maddie shook her head. What had just happened? She looked around and found her sisters rallying around her. Mrs. Poole had appeared with the green gown in her hands as Mrs. Selis and Mrs. Lance directed Maddie to the dressmaker's shop a few doors down on the square.

They dragged her inside and shut the door. Maddie looked at Mrs. Selis. "I don't know what just happened out there, but thank you."

"My pleasure," Mrs. Selis said. "I'm sure your dear mother would have a fit if she knew that you were going to declare your love looking like that."

"Declare my love?" Maddie swallowed her horror at the thought. "You mean this wasn't a diversionary tactic?"

Amelia was behind Maddie untying her work apron, while Mrs. Poole prepared the green gown.

"Of course you're still going to declare your love," Mrs. Selis said. "It's about time too. Why, to think you are portraying yourself as a fallen woman when this whole time you have actually been in love. What would your mother think?"

They yanked her gown off over her head and settled the green one on. "But I don't understand. I lied. I cheated. I broke everyone's hearts."

"You did what you thought was best for everyone involved. Now it's time to do what's best for you." Mrs. Selis brushed imaginary lint off the shoulder of the gown while her sisters buttoned her up. "There, now you look like the lady you really are." The older woman gave her a hug.

"Be brave and do what your heart tells you to do. Remember, the whole town is counting on you to do it right this time."

"No pressure there," Maddie muttered as she was pushed out the door. The women of the town had gathered near the door as a show of support. Maddie glanced up to see that Trevor strode down the street, flowers in hand, followed by the other suitors. He had a fierce look on his face and her heart tripped. Behind the suitors were the rest of the men in town, including the mayor, the sheriff and her father.

Trevor stopped two yards from where she stood on the wooden walkway in front of the shop.

"All right, Madeline," he said formally. "The rest of the men and I are ready to hear what is truly in your heart." Silence fell as everyone waited expectantly for her to speak.

Maddie swallowed and glanced at the ladies. They smiled and nodded their encouragement. "You all have been so kind to me," she started.

"Cut to the chase," the sheriff said. "Are you in love or aren't you?"

"Yes," she said, finding her courage. "I am in love."

"And are you in love with one of these gents or not?"

"Yes," she said and looked at the men. "I am in love with one of you."

"Who?" the crowd demanded.

Maddie's heart raced. Her palms began to sweat but she realized that it was now or never. "I am in love with Trevor Montgomery."

There was a gasp in the crowd and then a cheer. The men pounded Trevor on the back and congratulated him. Maddie stared at her toes. She couldn't stand to look at him. She didn't want to see his face when he told her and the whole town that he didn't return her love, couldn't return her love after what she did.

Then Trevor was in front of her. He took a gentle hold on her chin and raised her gaze to his. His dark eyes were filled with heat and promise and an emotion she had only dared to believe. "Madeline Morgan," he declared loud enough for the entire town to hear. "I love you too."

"What?" Maddie blinked.

He smiled and squeezed her hands. "I love you too. I think I loved you from the first moment I saw you standing there with that rifle in your hands." He got down on his knee. "Maddie, will you forsake all other suitors and marry me?"

Maddie's heart leaped in her chest. She took a deep breath, still uncertain that this whole scene was real.

"Yes," she said. "Yes Trevor, I will marry you."

"And forsake all other suitors," he reminded her.

She laughed and glanced around the crowd. "Yes, I will forsake all other suitors and marry you."

A cheer went up from the crowd. Trevor stood up and grabbed Maddie around the waist and twirled her. "Thank goodness," he whispered, eyes shining. "Thank goodness." Then he kissed her right there in front of the entire town. Maddie put her arms around his neck and kissed him back with all the emotion in her heart.

The pure joy and excitement of the moment muffled the sound of the crowd as they kissed. It took Mrs. Selis and Maddie's father to break them apart, but even then their hands remained together, fingers entwined.

"Come on everyone," Mrs. Selis said. "We have a lot to do. It looks like there's going to be a wedding after all."

They were married two days later in the small chapel at the end of Main Street. The whole town came to the wedding. There was a giant pot luck dinner and more dancing.

Maddie looked like a princess in the dress the ladies had made for her. She was careful not to stain or tear it. When the day was over, she would clean it and press it and put it away for the next lucky girl to wear the day she realized her dreams.